"I wouldn't mind getting out of this dress and these shoes," Kim said without thinking.

David gave her a lopsided grin, letting his gaze travel down to her feet and back up again.

"Don't get your hopes up." Too late, she realized how her remark might have sounded. "It's hot, and my feet hurt, that's all."

"Ah, here's the Kim we all know and love," he drawled. "You've been so nice to me today that you had me worried. I thought an alien had taken over your body."

"Better an alien than you." Instantly she wanted to bite her tongue. "I'm sorry."

He held up his hand. "No, no. I needed the reality check."

His wry grin sent shivers through her. More than anything, she wanted to throw her arms around him and kiss that clever mouth. Obviously what she desperately needed after all the enforced togetherness of the last hours was a breather.

Dear Reader,

Breeze into fall with six rejuvenating romances from Silhouette Special Edition! We are happy to feature our READERS' RING selection, *Hard Choices* (SE#1561), by favorite author Allison Leigh, who writes, "I wondered about the masks people wear, such as the 'good' girl/boy vs. the 'bad' girl/boy, and what ultimately hardens or loosens those masks. Annie and Logan have worn masks that don't fit, and their past actions wouldn't be considered ideal behavior. I hope readers agree this is a thought-provoking scenario!"

We can't get enough of Pamela Toth's WINCHESTER BRIDES miniseries as she delivers the next book, *A Winchester Homecoming* (SE#1562). Here, a world-weary heroine comes home only to find her former flame ready to reignite their passion. MONTANA MAVERICKS: THE KINGSLEYS returns with Judy Duarte's latest, *Big Sky Baby* (SE#1563). In this tale, a Kingsley cousin comes home to find that his best friend is pregnant. All of a sudden, he can't stop thinking of starting a family…with her!

Victoria Pade brings us an engagement of convenience and a passion of *in*convenience, in *His Pretend Fiancée* (SE#1564), the next book in the MANHATTAN MULTIPLES miniseries. Don't miss *The Bride Wore Blue Jeans* (SE#1565), the last in veteran Marie Ferrarella's miniseries, THE ALASKANS. In this heartwarming love story, a confirmed bachelor flies to Alaska and immediately falls for the woman least likely to marry! In *Four Days, Five Nights* (SE#1566) by Christine Flynn, two strangers are forced to face a growing attraction when their small plane crashes in the wilds.

These moving romances will foster discussion, escape and lots of daydreaming. Watch for more heart-thumping stories that show the joys and complexities of a woman's world.

Happy reading!

Karen Taylor Richman,
Senior Editor

Please address questions and book requests to:
Silhouette Reader Service
U.S.: 3010 Walden Ave., P.O. Box 1325, Buffalo, NY 14269
Canadian: P.O. Box 609, Fort Erie, Ont. L2A 5X3

A Winchester Homecoming

PAMELA TOTH

Silhouette®

SPECIAL EDITION™

Published by Silhouette Books

America's Publisher of Contemporary Romance

Dedicated to readers everywhere who are separated
from their loved ones, whatever the reason, with the
sincere hope that you find your way home again soon.

 SILHOUETTE BOOKS

ISBN 0-373-24562-9

A WINCHESTER HOMECOMING

Copyright © 2003 by Pamela Toth

All rights reserved. Except for use in any review, the reproduction
or utilization of this work in whole or in part in any form by any
electronic, mechanical or other means, now known or hereafter
invented, including xerography, photocopying and recording, or in
any information storage or retrieval system, is forbidden without
the written permission of the editorial office, Silhouette Books,
233 Broadway, New York, NY 10279 U.S.A.

All characters in this book have no existence outside the imagination of
the author and have no relation whatsoever to anyone bearing the same
name or names. They are not even distantly inspired by any individual
known or unknown to the author, and all incidents are pure invention.

This edition published by arrangement with Harlequin Books S.A.

® and TM are trademarks of Harlequin Books S.A., used under license.
Trademarks indicated with ® are registered in the United States Patent
and Trademark Office, the Canadian Trade Marks Office and in other
countries.

Visit Silhouette at www.eHarlequin.com

Printed in U.S.A.

PAMELA TOTH

USA TODAY bestselling author Pamela Toth was born in Wisconsin, but grew up in Seattle where she attended the University of Washington and majored in art. Now living on the Puget Sound area's east side, she has two daughters, Erika and Melody, and two Siamese cats.

Recently she took a lead from one of her romances and married her high school sweetheart, Frank. When she's not writing, she enjoys traveling with her husband, reading, playing FreeCell on the computer, doing counted cross-stitch and researching new story ideas. She's been an active member of Romance Writers of America since 1982.

She loves hearing from readers and can be reached at P.O. Box 5845, Bellevue, WA 98006. For a personal reply, a stamped, self-addressed envelope is appreciated.

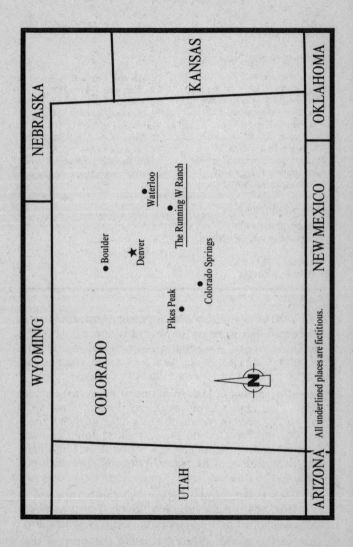

WYOMING

NEBRASKA

KANSAS

COLORADO

• Boulder

★ Denver

• Waterloo

The Running W Ranch

Pikes Peak
•

• Colorado Springs

UTAH

N

ARIZONA   All underlined places are fictitious.   NEW MEXICO   OKLAHOMA

Prologue

Kim Winchester stood frozen in the open stable doorway, her initial shock turning to disgust as she stared at the couple locked in a passionate embrace between the rows of stalls.

She had never dreamed he could act this way, too caught up in kissing the woman coiled around him like a snake to even *care* that his betrayal would break Kim's heart. He had insisted over and over how important she was to him, but right now it was clear he'd forgotten her very existence.

Tears filled Kim's eyes, but she refused to let them fall. She felt devastated and sick, but she had no intention of slinking away quietly and pretending she hadn't seen the two of them.

"Oh, isn't this just too, too cozy," she drawled, sauntering into the light as though she didn't have a care in the world, pleased beneath the hurt as the couple sprang apart. "You two make me want to barf."

She'd half expected to see a gleam of triumph in Emily's eyes, but instead the other woman looked totally mortified.

"Kim," she pleaded, eyes wide.

Kim ignored her entreaty. "I knew you were after him!" She shook an accusing finger in Emily's face. "I could tell by the way you practically drooled when we saw you in town." Did Emily think she was blind or just naive?

It was obvious that the older woman could think of nothing to say in her own defense, but Kim's feeling of vindication was immediately wiped away when *he* stepped in front of Emily. Protecting her.

He didn't look embarrassed. Quite the contrary. His thick brows were bunched into a thunderous frown, and he was glaring at Kim. Bristling with disapproval.

How could he be so mean, siding with this woman he barely knew, against his own daughter?

Chapter One

David Major was headed in the general direction of Denver with classic country cranked up on the stereo and the car windows rolled down to let in the rush of warm air. Idly he glanced at the fields of dried stubble on either side of the road, the barren expanse occasionally broken by a cluster of jutting buildings before it marched to the distant horizon. Each fancy new hotel complex, set well away from the main road and dwarfed by the empty prairie surrounding it, managed to appear as out of place in flat, rural Colorado as satin panties on a sow.

Who would have thought a decade ago when he'd first moved here from noisy, smelly, crowded L.A. that he'd grow to appreciate the open spaces, the distant mountains and the clean, dry air? That he'd find work he enjoyed and a home he loved on a cattle ranch, of all places?

Up ahead of him appeared the jagged line of man-made white peaks that topped the Denver airport terminal. They were supposed to symbolize the Rocky Mountains, but looked instead more like a row of oversize canvas teepees than anything found in nature.

Adam Winchester had broken his leg the day before, so David was here in his stepfather's place to meet Kim's plane from Seattle. It was hard to believe that she'd been David's first real friend in Waterloo, where he'd felt as out of place at the rural school as a sports car at a tractor pull, or to remember that at sixteen he'd been on the brink of a hormone-driven adolescent crush. She had looked beyond his dyed hair and bizarre clothes, much to her father's initial horror, and befriended him.

Their bond had been broken when she'd left a few months later without saying goodbye, to live with the mother she barely knew. Since her father had married David's mother, Kim was technically his stepsister, but he'd only seen her a couple of times over the years. The woman he was meeting today was a stranger. He just hoped her flight was on time.

He followed the sign directing him to visitor parking and speculated on how her appearance might have changed in the five years since he'd seen her. Did her dark hair still fall past her shoulders? Was her figure still slim? Not that he cared, except that picking her out of a crowd would be easier if she hadn't colored her hair or put on a lot of weight.

He parked the car, which he'd borrowed from Adam instead of driving his own pickup truck, and headed for the terminal and baggage claim. Would she be disappointed to see him waiting for her instead of her father? Of course she would, even though her visits home had been few and she'd always come without her husband, the overworked preppy attorney.

David wondered why she was here now, and traveling alone once more. He hadn't asked Adam how long she was staying. Not his business.

Following a young family through the doors into the slightly cooler main terminal, he allowed himself one bit of curiosity. Would Kim treat him like an old friend or the stranger she'd made sure he had become?

Kim doubted that she had ever been so tired in her life. It seemed as though she'd been exhausted ever since she and Drew had first separated over three months before. She went to bed tired, but she didn't sleep all that long or well, so she woke up tired, too. Just getting through the day wore her out, even though she didn't do much. She supposed that she would have to find a job when she got home, but she hadn't even started looking. Maybe the clean, dry air of Colorado would revitalize her, restore her spirit.

Heal her.

She hadn't yet told her father that she'd left Drew, which she had convinced herself wasn't the kind of news you gave over the phone or in an e-mail. Of course it also relieved her of having to make explanations. Between her husband and his family, she'd already had enough drama to last for a lifetime. When she'd called to ask her father if she could come home for a while, he hadn't even wanted to know why.

If he'd been curious, he'd kept it under wraps, just

as he always had hidden his feelings behind a stern mask. After Kim's mother left, he had been a single parent to Kim. When she became a teenager he still treated her like a child, so they had frequently butted heads. Since his marriage to David's mother, Emily, he had started opening up, but for Kim it had been too little, too late.

She would have to admit, at least to herself, though, that he was always there for her when she needed him. Until now she just hadn't allowed herself to need him.

She smothered a yawn behind her hand as she marched up the toasty warmth of the jet way and headed toward the baggage area. For once she actually looked forward to her father's reticence, if it meant that he wouldn't pelt her with questions all the way home.

Tears misted her eyes as she walked. To be fair, his quiet strength was just what she needed.

For the first fifteen years of her life, he had been her entire world. Then she'd walked in on him with Emily. Jealousy and betrayal had sent Kim running to the mother she hardly knew. Pride and obligation kept her there until she broke away and married Drew.

Absently Kim touched the scar on her cheekbone. She had paid for her choices, but part of her still felt guilty for hurting her father. On her wedding day, he had unbent enough to say he loved her, but he hadn't said he was proud of her. At least now she had outgrown the need for anyone's stamp of approval, but it was still nice to be home.

Stopping to hunt for a tissue in her shoulder bag, she didn't immediately scan the waiting crowd for her father's tall figure, perhaps topped by the Reba cap Kim sent him last Christmas.

"You cut your hair."

The voice at her elbow made her jump. Her head jerked up, snapping her teeth together. She stared into a pair of familiar brown eyes as her fingers strayed to the short hair at her neck.

"Where's Daddy?" Exhaustion and disappointment combined to make Kim's tone sharper than she had intended, but she didn't try to soften it. As she looked past David Major, he shifted his weight from one hip to the other and pushed back the brim of his Stetson. His smug expression made her bristle. How long had he been watching her search the crowd for her father?

Cowboy wannabe, she thought with a mental curl of her lip.

"Adam couldn't make it," David drawled, rocking back on the heels of his boots and tucking his thumbs into his belt. The buckle, she noticed, was a flashy silver oval, probably something he'd won at a local rodeo. At least it didn't have his initial outlined in turquoise stones.

Since she knew darned well David had spent his formative years in southern California, she wanted to ask where the drawl had come from. Before she could, his words registered and a band of fear closed around her throat like a hangman's noose.

Her father wouldn't have disappointed her, not if he had a choice.

"What do you mean, he couldn't 'make it'?" she mimicked, hiding her concern. If there was anything she'd learned over the past few years, it was the wisdom of keeping her emotions hidden. She must not have been entirely successful, because David's cool expression relaxed slightly and he touched her shoulder with his hand. Before she could prevent herself, she stiffened and pulled away.

Immediately his expression hardened again.

"Don't worry," he said gruffly. "Adam broke his leg yesterday, that's all. The doc says it's clean, just a hairline fracture, but he didn't think the ride here would help any." For a moment, a grin tugged at David's mouth. "Not that Adam didn't do his damnedest to change Doc's mind, but he didn't stand a chance once Mom got involved."

Part of Kim's mind resented his proprietary comment about *her* father. David wasn't even related, except by his mother's marriage into the Winchester family. Was he trying to show Kim that she didn't belong here anymore?

"How did he break it?" She ignored his smile. "And don't tell me Daddy was thrown from a horse. I wouldn't believe that if I'd been away for a hundred years." The horse that could unseat Adam Winchester hadn't yet been foaled.

By unspoken consent, she and David had both started walking toward the baggage carousel that was already spitting out a steady stream of luggage, cardboard cartons girded with tape and various pieces of sporting equipment.

"It was actually one of the new ranch hands who got thrown," David explained. "He managed to land square on Adam and knock him down. The rest, as they say, is history."

She stopped to gape at David. "Daddy must have been furious."

"Livid. Turned the air blue." David's gaze was

on the carousel, his chiseled profile a sharp reminder of how much he had changed. The cute boy had become a ruggedly attractive man, and this was the longest conversation she'd had with him in years. Good thing she was immune.

"Which one is yours?" he asked without bothering to glance her way.

His disinterest reminded her that she, too, had changed. Besides her chopped-off hair, she'd lost weight. Not a bad thing, since Drew had been telling her she was getting too fat, but now her slacks and top hung on her and there were probably circles under her eyes, right next to the fairly recent scar on her cheek.

Lovely. Not that she cared what David thought, anyway.

Kim searched the carousel and then she pointed. "That big one and those two by the skis."

His dark brows lifted. "Three bags?" He didn't try to hide his smirk. "Gee, is this all?"

"For now." Head high, she walked toward the exit, the fingers of one hand wrapped tightly around the strap of her shoulder purse as she left him to struggle with her luggage. Served him right for thinking she was a clotheshorse.

As soon as she'd taken a dozen steps, her burst of bravado was replaced with a new wave of exhaustion. Feeling dizzy, she sank gratefully into an empty chair and let her head fall back.

"What's wrong? Are you sick?" David demanded as he caught up with her and dumped her bags to the floor.

Opening her eyes or answering was too much of an effort, as was shaking her head.

"Stay here," he ordered her in a bossy tone. "Put your head between your knees if you feel nauseated. I'll find you some water."

Panic swirled around her. "No!" she finally croaked out, forcing open her eyes. Relieved to focus on his concerned face. "Don't leave me."

She hadn't meant to say that. Biting her lip in self-punishment, she watched his expression change from concern to something more difficult to read. Angry tears over her slip blurred her vision, but she blinked them away and glared up at him.

Immediately he squatted down next to her chair, his gaze level with hers as he took her hand in his larger, stronger one. His warmth was a welcome surprise. She was so cold, always cold.

"Your hand is like ice!" he exclaimed.

She pulled away from his loose grasp. "It must be the air-conditioning in here. They always overdo it."

"Actually, it's fairly warm," he contradicted. "When's the last time you had anything to eat?"

"On the plane."

He leaned closer. "Kim, what's wrong with you?"

She wondered if he realized it was the first time he'd called her by name since she arrived.

"I cut my hair several years ago," she said, hoping to distract him with a reply to his initial question. "It was just too much of a nuisance, and long hair's gone out of style on the coast." It wasn't really true, but he wouldn't know that.

She'd hacked it off to pay back Drew for being overly friendly with a short-haired paralegal in his office. He'd been furious and he had, of course, retaliated against Kim's rebelliousness. Besting him, however briefly, had nearly been worth it, even though she'd never worn the yellow diamond pendant he'd eventually bought her as a peace offering. It had gone into her jewelry drawer, along with several other nice pieces she had acquired under similar circumstances.

Nor had she ever grown her hair long again, despite Drew's insistence. But of course she didn't tell David any of that while his unreadable gaze stayed on her like some kind of laser.

"Water would be nice," she said when he didn't comment. "Chilled, if you don't mind, and bottled, not tap water."

He straightened, a shutter sliding down over his expression, and tugged at his hat brim in a gesture she figured was more mocking than polite. "I'll be right back. Stay here with the bags."

She watched him walk through the crowd, his long strides eating up the distance to the nearest vendor, as if he couldn't get away from her fast enough.

Well, why should he be any different? she asked herself silently on another trembling note of self-pity. What was there about Kim Winchester Sterling for anyone to like or admire?

As usual, not one thing came to her tired mind.

After Kim had gulped down the chilled bottled water David brought her and surprised him by stepping out of her ice-princess role long enough to thank him, he escorted her out to the car. She had spurned his suggestion of a wheelchair and he, in turn, had refused her offer to help with her bags. As he stacked two of them and hiked the strap of the third on his shoulder, she dug sunglasses out from her purse and slipped them on like a shield to hide behind.

"I'll bet the weather seems different from what you're used to," he said conversationally as he wheeled the largest bags behind them.

"I grew up here, remember?" She pressed her lips together and turned away, as if she regretted her comment.

"I haven't forgotten," he replied. He might have said more, but instead he let the silence hang between them for a moment. When she didn't lift her head, he shifted the bag on his shoulder and kept walking.

On the drive back to the ranch, he thought she might ask about her father or their mutual half brother, Jake, who was nine, and sister, Cheyenne, eight, or the rest of her extended family, but she didn't.

"The old church on Dammer Road burned down," he volunteered, his gaze on the road ahead. "They're rebuilding already, brick instead of wood this time."

Her response was a noncommittal hum in her throat as she looked out the window. Frustrated, David fell silent. She had grown up in Elbert County, but if she wanted news, she would have to ask.

Traffic wasn't especially heavy and the road didn't demand much of his attention, which left him free to speculate about the reason for Kim's visit, her first in several years, and to wonder about the absence of a wedding ring. Perhaps she had lost it or was having it repaired or just didn't wear one. Unlike some women with successful husbands, she wasn't flashing a lot of fancy jewelry.

Back in school she had been a pretty girl with a warm smile and a budding figure. Now her face was all cheekbones and angles, big green eyes behind the tinted lenses and a scar she kept touching with her fingertip. Slim tan pants and a long-sleeved pink shirt made her look thinner. Her short hair bared her neck and ears.

He'd stuck his tongue in her ear once, but she had squealed and pulled away, embarrassing them both. He liked to think his technique had improved since then.

She'd had issues when he'd known her before, rebelliousness against her father's strictness, possessiveness of the only parent she'd known up till then and jealousy of David's mother. He had figured Kim found what she had needed in Seattle, but now he wondered.

For a woman who had it all, she seemed more brittle than content, and she looked tired. Remembering how she had once bothered to search behind his own prickly shell, he tried again.

"Did you know that Cornell Hobbs and Bonnie Gill finally tied the knot?" he asked. "They've been together since high school, so it was no surprise."

When she didn't answer, he glanced in her direction, expecting to see her staring out the side window with a bored expression. Instead her head had tipped forward. Her eyes were closed, her full lips slightly parted, and the rise and fall of her breasts was slow and regular.

Apparently, his fascinating conversation had lulled her right to sleep.

The gentle bumping of the car across the cattle guard at the entrance to Winchester land woke Kim from a jumble of dreams. She took a deep breath and sneaked a glance at David, but he was looking at the

Appaloosas grazing in the near pasture. Whenever she saw a horse with the breed's distinctive markings, she thought of her father and the ranch.

"You okay?" David asked as he slowed to allow a Jeep to pass from the other direction and returned the driver's wave.

Her first reply was a rusty croak, so she cleared her throat and tried again. "Yes, I'm fine. Thanks for meeting my plane."

"No problem."

They passed a traditional two-story farmhouse, painted light blue with fresh white trim. The backyard jungle gym was new, as was the weather vane on the roof. The familiar riot of brightly blooming pots and hanging baskets on the wide front porch was a testament to Aunt Rory's green thumb, but the driveway in front of the matching garage was empty.

Kim was relieved that they didn't have to stop and say hello to Uncle Travis and his brood. There would be time enough to visit later, after she had reassured herself that her father was really all right except for his leg.

She couldn't wrap her mind around the image of him on crutches. He was too powerful for that, too strong, just like the large immovable boulder in the northeast section of the range.

"Mom's cleaned your old room for you," David added as he took the fork in the road that would lead them to the big house where Kim had grown up. "She and Adam are looking forward to seeing you."

The idea that Emily would be as eager as Kim's father to see her was ludicrous. Although the two women got along, they weren't close.

Was David sending up a trial balloon to test Kim?

To deduce what her attitude toward his mother might be?

"That was nice of Emily," she replied quietly, slipping off her sunglasses and tucking them into her purse. They had been expensive, but she couldn't seem to care whether or not they got scratched.

The light glinted off her birthstone ring. Self-consciously she touched the bare spot where her platinum wedding set had been, wondering if David had noticed its absence.

Drew certainly had when she'd first removed it. He had gone ballistic.

Determinedly Kim pushed aside the memory as the car rounded the familiar last curve. Despite her catnap, she was still tired. Maybe she would have time for a real rest before dinner. Even though her dad and Emily had two more kids, they'd kept Kim's bedroom available for her. It was the one refuge in the large house that hadn't been taken over by her stepmother.

"Are you still living at the Johnson place?" she asked David. Even though Emily had bought the small spread from Ed Johnson when she and David first came to town and it had since become part of the Running W, everyone still referred to it by the name of its previous owner and probably always would.

"Yep." He turned into the wide driveway and pulled up next to a bike lying on its side.

Toys had never been left out when Kim was small. Fighting the mixed emotions crowding up into her throat, she unbuckled her seat belt with hands that trembled. Swallowing hard, she focused on her simple relief at being here. All the rest—the questions,

the explanations, the decisions she needed to make—
could be sorted through and dealt with later. For
now, she would just *enjoy.*

Even though David hadn't honked, the front door
burst open and her half brother and sister spilled out
as though they had been watching through the window. They were followed by her father on his
crutches.

The sight of him brought tears to Kim's eyes. He
was bareheaded, his thick, black hair laced with more
silver than she remembered. His face, creased now
by a wide grin, was weathered by a life spent out of
doors. Hunched slightly over his crutches, he appeared older than he had the last time she'd seen him,
when he had insisted on flying out to Seattle for her
birthday.

Hovering at his elbow was Emily, looking trim
and perky. She even managed to appear pleased by
the arrival of her uninvited houseguest.

Instantly the snide thought made Kim feel guilty.
As always, Emily's smile was cordial. Even after
Kim's outburst in the stable when she'd caught the
two of them making out like teenagers and her father
had been so angry at her, Emily had pretended to be
understanding. If she had done so to impress her new
boyfriend with her niceness, it had certainly worked.

Kim had desperately needed his reassurance, so
she'd lashed out like a jealous lover. When he'd
taken Emily's side against her, she'd been totally humiliated. The memory of her bratty attitude still embarrassed her, but the important thing was that Emily
made him happy.

Kim would have to try harder to like Emily while

she was here. Her father would be pleased to see the two of them getting along.

"Hi, Kim!"

Jake and Cheyenne's headlong dash and noisy greetings reminded Kim a little of her mother-in-law's cocker spaniels. She dragged up a big smile, feeling as though her cheeks would split.

"Hey, how are you two?" she asked, holding out her arms.

They'd both grown a lot since the last time she had seen them. Cheyenne, blond like her mother, threw her arms around Kim in an exuberant hug. Jake, with their father's dark hair, skidded to a stop, hands jammed into his pockets. With a young boy's wariness, he appeared ready to bolt if Kim even tried to hug him. She patted his head instead and he rewarded her restraint with a grin.

"How long are you staying?" Cheyenne demanded, grabbing her hand.

The blunt question caught Kim by surprise. She hadn't thought that far ahead.

"Why don't you and Jake help me with the bags while she says hi to your folks?" David suggested, opening the trunk.

Kim's attention turned to her father who'd been waiting patiently.

"Hey, princess," he said, balancing on one crutch as he held out his free hand.

"Hi, Daddy." With a little sigh of relief, she wrapped her arms around his waist while he gave her an awkward hug. When he let her go, she and Emily exchanged air kisses near each other's cheeks.

"Welcome home," Emily said gently.

Kim's guilt increased tenfold. She had stopped being jealous years ago, and Emily was way nicer than her own mother, so what was Kim's problem other than a whisper of disloyalty?

Before she could puzzle it out, David and the younger kids joined them with the bags.

"I guess you didn't have any trouble finding her," her father said to him.

"I haven't changed that much!" Kim protested.

"You're thinner," her father replied with typical male bluntness and a frown she knew stemmed from concern.

His implied criticism still stung, making her cheeks go hot with embarrassment.

"Some people say a woman can't be too thin or too rich," Emily commented smoothly, dispelling the awkward moment with a hostess's effortless smile. "Come inside, Kim, and we'll get you settled."

Even though she appreciated Emily's tact, part of Kim felt like insisting that she would rather stay outside, just to be contrary. And maybe she could throw herself down in the driveway and drum her heels on the pavement, just to show her maturity.

"Thank you," she said instead.

"You might like a nap before dinner," Emily continued. "It's just the five of us tonight." She glanced at David. "Unless you'd like to join us, honey?"

To Kim's relief, he shook his head. "Thanks, Mom, but I've got stuff to do back at my place."

Kim's father patted her shoulder before his hands returned to the grips on his crutches, his gaze steady on hers. "I'm glad you're here, Kimmie," he said quietly.

"Me, too." Her chin wobbled, so she turned away to give David a bright, blank smile. "Would you mind taking my bags up to my room before you leave?''

''Sure thing, *princess*,'' he drawled with a mocking grin.

Ignoring his jab, Kim followed her father up the front steps. Despite his height and bum leg, he took them with surprising agility, but he'd always been a natural athlete.

Feeling a little like a spectator at a play about family dynamics—or perhaps a TV sitcom—David hitched up the strap of Kim's shoulder bag as Jake and Cheyenne both began tugging on the handle of the wheeled suitcase. To head off a skirmish, David dug his keys from his pocket.

''Who wants to lock the car?'' he asked, dangling them like the proverbial carrot.

Both kids missed the irony of his question. The chance of anyone stealing the sedan from the boss's driveway was right up there with the likelihood of the two kids being able to get the heavy suitcases up the stairs. Kim must have it filled it with rocks from Puget Sound.

Jake's hand shot up first. ''I'll do it!''

When David tossed him the keys, which he caught with a triumphant shout, Cheyenne's eyes filled with tears.

Thinking fast, David grabbed the handle of the largest suitcase. ''Honey bun, would you hold the front door open for me?''

The brewing thundercloud on her face was replaced by instant sunshine. She was going to be a heartbreaker. As her oldest sibling, he would have to stay in shape just to keep the boys in line.

The idea of testosterone-driven adolescent males

sniffing around her at some point in the not-too-distant future was enough to make his head ache.

"Sure thing," she crowed, running up the steps.

Jake opened his mouth, but David froze him with a warning stare. "Don't lose my keys," David told him, turning away.

He might be a childless bachelor, but he'd spent enough time baby-sitting his half siblings to learn a few tricks, he thought as he noticed that his mother was waiting for him in the entryway.

"Nicely done," she said after he had thanked Cheyenne for holding the door and she had skipped ahead.

"You taught me all I know," he replied, shifting the bag on his shoulder. A fresh flower arrangement sat on a side table, no doubt from her own garden. Adam and Kim had gone into the spacious living room. "I'd better get these right up to sis's room, in case she needs them in the next couple of minutes."

His mother smothered a chuckle. "Behave yourself," she scolded softly. "And you know the two of you aren't actually related."

"Thank God," he muttered back, leaning down to peck her cheek. He rolled the suitcase across the tiled floor. "I'll come back for this." Once he had, he planned to sneak out through the kitchen.

He would have liked to say something encouraging to his mother, since he knew how hard she worked at being the perfect stepparent. It burned him to no end that she blamed herself for coming between Adam and his daughter and sending her away. It wasn't true.

"Kim!" Adam exclaimed from the living room,

the urgency in his voice drawing both David's and his mother's attention.

He turned in time to see Adam struggling to his feet as Kim slid gracefully to the floor.

"Is she dead?" Cheyenne shrieked as David dropped the suitcase and ducked around his mother.

"No, dear," Emily replied calmly. "I think she's fainted."

Adam's frustration at his temporary limitations was easy to read on his contorted face. "Kim!" he shouted again.

When David bent over her, she was as pale as milk, but already her eyes were beginning to flutter open. The others gathered around to see if she was all right as David bent down and scooped her into his arms. Compared to bucking hay bales and wrestling livestock, lifting her was easy. He was surprised at how little she weighed. No wonder she'd gone down like a heart-shot buck.

"I'm fine," she insisted, already starting to struggle. "Put me down!"

He was about to make some smart-alecky comment in order to lighten the tension when he got a look at her face. He'd expected to see confusion, embarrassment, perhaps even annoyance at the proprietary way he had hauled her up. What he read instead in her wide green eyes made him set her carefully back onto her feet.

In the instant before she managed to hide it, her face had been filled with fear.

Chapter Two

"I told you calling a doctor wasn't necessary." The irritation in Kim's tone when she spoke to her father was a ruse intended to cover her embarrassment. "She said all I need is a nap."

Emily had gone back downstairs to show the doctor out, and Kim's father sat on the edge of her bed, his crutches propped up next to him and his callused hand covering hers.

"You fainted. What Dr. Wilson actually said was that you haven't been taking very good care of yourself, so you're dehydrated and probably exhausted."

His tone was bland, but the concern in his eyes only increased Kim's guilt. He probably deserved an explanation, one she wasn't yet ready to give. She had gotten herself into this mess and it was her fault, all of it, but what she wanted to do right now was to regroup in the familiar surroundings from her youth.

"Like I told you," she replied, "a rest and some water will fix me right up."

She jutted her chin, gaze daring him to argue. For a moment she thought he'd push it as he assessed her.

The unyielding expression on his weathered face brought back so many memories of her frustration in dealing with him, of rebellious youth butting up against parental authority, of tears and tantrums on her part and refusal to bend on his.

Then he patted her hand, positioned his crutches and pulled himself to his feet. Just coming upstairs must have been a real struggle for him, she realized with a stab of remorse.

"I'm glad you're here, Kimmie," he said as he found his balance.

"Me, too." Relief washed over her. Eyes misting, she managed a shaky smile, hoping it would ease his concern. "Thanks, Daddy."

"Anytime. You know that," he said gruffly. "Emily's bringing you up some soup. If there's anything else you need…" His voice trailed off, an open invitation for her to confide in him, but she wasn't ready to lay out her mistakes.

"I'll be fine, really," she said.

Still he hovered. "I'll see you in the morning, then." He frowned at his leg as though it had deliberately let him down by allowing itself to get broken. "Emily won't let me come back up here tonight."

As if on cue, his wife appeared in the doorway carrying a tray.

"I feel useless," he grumbled when he looked at her.

"Knock it off," she responded cheerfully. "That hangdog expression isn't fooling anyone, and I know you'd whisk the tray right out of my hands if you could."

Husband and wife exchanged meaningful glances that told Kim they'd be discussing her later. She hoped they wouldn't tell her aunts and uncles that she had collapsed in the living room.

It was bad enough that her stepbrother had been here to see her swoon like a Victorian maiden, worse that he was the one to lug her up the stairs with no more concern than a bag of feed. As her head cleared, she'd become too aware of his strength and her own vulnerability. The big show-off hadn't even been breathing hard when he'd laid her on the narrow bed with its ruffled coverlet, but their gazes had locked for an instant before he straightened to flash her a mocking grin.

"I knew you were faking," he'd whispered.

Now Emily set the tray across Kim's lap. "How are you feeling?" she asked brightly.

"Better, thank you." Kim glanced down at the steaming bowl of soup. As the appetizing aroma teased her nostrils, her mouth began to water.

"It's homemade chicken and noodle," Emily said as she transferred a small pitcher of ice water and an empty glass to the nightstand. "I had some in the freezer and I remembered that you liked it the last time you were here."

That was surprising, since Kim hadn't been home in five years. "It was nice of you to fix it for me."

Emily glanced over her shoulder at Kim's father,

who hovered in the doorway. He must be waiting for Emily to help him down the stairs. Knowing how independent he usually was, Kim was surprised that he hadn't just barreled ahead without assistance, even if it meant falling on his hard head. Risk had never slowed him down before, not that Kim could remember, but he'd sure blown up when he caught *her* riding on the back of David's motor scooter, even though she had been wearing a helmet.

Emily clasped her hands together and leaned closer. "This is your home, dear," she said quietly. "It always was, and it always will be."

"I know that." Kim's voice faltered. Spreading the napkin beneath her chin, she blinked rapidly to prevent herself from bursting into tears and embarrassing herself even more than she already had.

"You'd better go help Daddy before he gets tired of waiting and falls down the stairs." Wasn't one patient enough for the woman to flutter over?

If Emily was offended by the abrupt dismissal, she didn't show it. Instead she smiled patiently.

"Eat your soup before it gets cold and then have some rest. I'll check on you again later to see if you need anything else."

Before Emily had reached the doorway, Kim was already spooning up the soup. It was the first time she could remember being hungry in a long while.

From the landing at the base of the staircase, David watched Adam's slow, careful descent. David itched to help him, but the rancher's thunderous glare was a good indication that any offer of assistance would be forcefully rejected.

"I'm here to break his fall," David's mom joked,

her hand on the curved wood banister as she reached the landing ahead of him. She must have realized that trying to keep him downstairs after Kim's collapse would have been a waste of her breath, because she hadn't objected when he'd gone up earlier.

She was the only person David knew who was completely unfazed by the force of Adam's personality. He didn't lose his temper often, but his intimidating stare was enough to make anyone who was thinking about crossing him reconsider immediately.

Anyone except his wife. Once, he'd stated dryly that the reason he laid down the law was so she would have something to step on.

"If you think you're going to cushion me, you'd better put on some weight pretty damn quick," he growled now in response to her comment about breaking his fall.

"Thank you, sweetie." Her voice was teasing as he thumped down the stairs next to her. "You always know just what to say."

Dressed in light-green shorts and a sleeveless print blouse, she was still as slim and pretty as she'd been when she'd relocated her newly divorced self and her hostile, defensive son from L.A.

To David she'd always been the most beautiful mom in the world, even when he was angry over being dragged away from everything that was familiar. Despite a few gray strands mixed in with the honey blond, and faint smile lines bracketing her mouth, she was still gorgeous. Adam must think so, too, from the way he was ogling her. Although the awareness between them still made David uncomfortable, he envied what they had found together.

His biological father, a hotshot entertainment attorney, had made a big mistake in trading his mom in for a younger model. That marriage hadn't lasted very long, despite the early arrival of David's half brother, Zane. Its demise had been quickly followed by wife number three, who was only a few years older than David. By now she, too, had probably joined the ex-wives' club. Not that he would know, since he had finally stopped returning his father's infrequent calls.

"How's the princess doing?" David asked after Adam braced himself with one hand on the newel post.

"Who really knows?" He shrugged, nearly losing one of his crutches.

David figured the only way his mom was going to get Adam off his bum leg would be if David went home.

"I've got animals to tend to, so I'll see you in the morning," he said.

Technically, Adam was his boss. Over the years they had developed an easy working relationship that usually started with coffee at the bunkhouse with the other men. Since Adam's little accident, David had been dropping by here instead.

"Did you want to say goodbye?" His mother glanced upward. "She's probably still awake."

"No, that's okay." He'd had enough of Kim's company for one day. "I'm sure I'll run into her again soon."

Too soon.

"Thanks again for going to the airport for me," Adam told him.

"No problem." Excusing himself, David followed

his mother toward the back of the house where he'd parked his truck.

"Call me if you need anything," he told her when they got to the kitchen.

"Let me give you some of the casserole," she replied. "I made extra."

"You always do." He leaned against the granite counter while she dished up a generous portion into a plastic container. When she added four homemade dinner rolls and a big piece of apple pie, he didn't protest. Eating his own cooking was one of the many prices of "baching it" that he willingly paid in exchange for having his own place, but he wasn't about to turn down a meal he didn't have to cook.

"Was Kim very talkative when you picked her up today?" she asked innocently as she loaded the food into a small box.

David straightened away from the counter and helped himself to one of the sourdough rolls. "Not really. I already told you she nearly keeled over while we were going to the car, though." Devouring the roll in two bites, he took the box out of his mother's hands. "What exactly did you think she might say?"

She held open the screen door for him. "Oh, nothing. I was just curious."

He didn't push it, partly because he wasn't all that interested and partly because he didn't want to risk her taking back the pie. Instead he leaned down to kiss her cheek.

"I'll be working on the bathroom, but I'll hear the phone if you need to call." Since he had decided to remodel the master bath in the old rambler, he was eager to get the room finished and put back together.

She waited on the deck while he backed the truck around, and then she gave him a final wave. He glanced up at Kim's room, but all he could see was the lacy curtains blowing in the open window. He wondered how she felt about being home again after so long.

A few moments later David drove his one big splurge out the front gate. The house he shared with a dog and a one-eyed cat was only five minutes down the main road. As much as David loved every member of his extended family-by-marriage, living by himself gave him the breathing space he'd realized he needed when he'd come back after graduation from Colorado State.

The old rambler where he had lived for the past few years had been well built by the original owner. Updating it was a work in progress that often seemed to David like more *work* than *progress,* since he was doing most of it himself.

His mother had bought the property without realizing that it nearly bisected the neighboring cattle ranch, which just happened to belong to Adam and his two younger brothers. After she had married him, the little rambler sat empty until David reclaimed it.

As he drove slowly down his driveway, Lulu came running out to meet him. Because of his Aunt Robin's weakness for strays, he owned what had to be one of the ugliest dogs in all of Colorado. Lulu was part Airedale, part Lab, and the rest was anyone's guess.

Good thing she had big brown eyes and a great personality.

"Hey, Lulu." He got out of the truck, holding the box of food and the mail he had stopped to collect out of her reach with one hand as he patted her head with the other.

Her short coat was an unfortunate mixture of wiry black and brown waves, like a perm and dye job gone wrong, but her eyes brimmed with intelligence, and her loyalty was as solid as the hand-hewed beams of his house.

Thrilled to have him home, Lulu followed him up the steps to the wide front porch. The boards he'd used to replace those weakened by time and weather felt solid beneath his booted feet. Calvin, his cat, sat on the new railing and washed one orange paw, ignoring the arrival of his master as only a cat could.

''Hello to you, too,'' David said in passing.

Just to annoy Calvin, the dog poked her muzzle against his fur and blew out a noisy breath, then barely managed to dodge the retaliatory swipe of claws as Calvin laid his ears flat to his head and spat.

''Behave, you two,'' David scolded absently as the cat jumped down, still growling low in his throat, and followed them inside. What a ragtag parade they must make.

David took the food his mother had sent home with him straight through to the kitchen and set the box on the counter he'd redone in ceramic tile two winters before, after he and Karen Sanchez quit hanging out together. With a considering look at both animals, he picked the box back up, set it inside the cold oven and closed the door. No point in taking unnecessary chances.

Not with his mother's cooking.

Flipping through his mail, he took a beer from the refrigerator, popped the top and poured a good part of it down his throat. He figured limo duty to the airport and back had earned him a brew or two.

There was nothing in his mail except a couple of bills, a home repair magazine and a check for a saddle he'd sold. Sipping the rest of the beer more slowly, he grabbed a baseball cap and went back outside. He crossed the yard and driveway that separated the house from his mother's old studio. Beyond the small structure where she had restored rare books were the stable and corrals.

A breeze had come up to stir the hot, dry air, so he leaned on the fence that separated him from his horses and watched them graze while Lulu plunked her butt down beside him, panting softly.

David didn't usually dwell on the past, but Kim's arrival had stirred up a slew of memories. For a long time he had blamed the move to Waterloo on his parents' divorce, and he had blamed *that* on his mother. Eventually he'd figured out that a combination of things had brought them here and that David himself had been at least partially responsible.

Mothers tended to freak out when you got expelled for taking a gun to school, even when it belonged to your father and you'd only borrowed it for self-protection after being shot at by someone you refused to identify when you were out jogging.

It hadn't been his fault that some dude from a different high school thought David had been hassling his girl, which he hadn't. Before he knew what was happening, his mother had decided L.A. was no longer safe, so she had bought the Johnson place, a baby-blue pickup truck and a Stetson with a flowered band.

Well, maybe he was wrong about the hat.

What followed was too-cool teen rebel meets rural hicks and hayseeds. The local kids had taken one look at David's dyed orange hair with the sides shaved, his pierced ear and retro wardrobe, and avoided him like a bad case of hoof rot.

While he put aside the memories and drained the last of his beer, one of his mares moseyed close enough to see if he'd brought her any carrots. Polly was marked like one of Adam's Appaloosas, but she was actually a breed called Colorado Rangers.

"Sorry, girl." He rubbed her outstretched nose. "Maybe next time."

Her colt, a miniature copy of its spotted dam, approached David warily, its scruff of a tail flipping comically while its ears swiveled back and forth.

Lulu started to rise, so David signaled her with his free hand. She obeyed instantly, haunches lowering back down to the ground, but the slight movement had already spooked the colt. With a squeal of apprehension, Bandit spun away on spindly legs, followed at a more matronly pace by his mama. She looked back at David reproachfully.

"See what you did?" he teased Lulu. "Come on. Time for dinner."

After he had fed his furry roommates, putting Calvin's dish up where Lulu couldn't reach it, he set about microwaving the casserole for his own dinner. Usually eating alone didn't bother him, but tonight when he sat down at the table, the silence seemed hollow instead of peaceful. Refusing to analyze his feelings, he got up and turned on the TV news so that voices filled the room while he finished his meal.

* * *

Kim glanced around self-consciously as she followed her father out of the school auditorium where Sunday services were being held until the new church on Dammer Road was completed. She'd forgotten how most of the congregation always stayed around outside afterward, weather permitting, in order to show off their nice clothes and visit with their friends while their kids ran loose.

The Winchesters were no different. All of them, right down to Uncle Charlie's new baby in a pink lace dress and booties, were slicked out in their Sunday best.

While Kim stood hugging herself and wishing she was back in her room, unchanged since she'd been a teenager, an elderly rancher in a Stetson and a bolo tie approached her father. He had reminded Emily twice on the drive over that he had a doctor appointment first thing tomorrow, and Kim knew he was counting on being able to ditch his crutches.

"Not without a written note," Emily had retorted as she parked the car.

A pregnant woman with two toddlers in tow greeted Emily as Jake and Cheyenne joined a group of children in a noisy game of tag. After an hour of sitting still, they had energy to burn. Kim's cousin Steve and another boy his age were ignoring two girls who strolled by in minis and cropped tops. One of them tossed back her streaked blond hair and they both giggled.

How was it possible that little Stevie was old enough to be interested in girls?

Kim raised tentative fingers to her own short hair. The last time she'd been here, it had been long and straight. She'd worn it that same way all through school.

Despite her father's strictness, she'd always had a lot of friends, taking her popularity for granted. When David came along, so different from the kids she'd known all her life, she'd felt sorry for him. Soon the two of them were friends and allies.

Now that was all changed, their friendship, her ability to fit in and certainly her confidence. Seeing Steve and his buddies made her feel old and worn-out at twenty-five.

She resisted the urge to touch the scar she had covered with concealer, fiddling instead with the belt of her rose-pink dress. At least the fitted style turned the weight she'd dropped into an asset, but she still felt a wave of unexpected shyness as she darted glances at the knots of people scattered across the expanse of dry brown lawn. Most of them she remembered, of course, but she wondered if anyone recognized her behind her trendy sunglasses.

Melinda Snodgrass, a girl Kim had never liked, was walking purposefully in her direction. Before Kim could figure out an escape, one of her aunts headed Melinda off. The same thing happened when a young couple from her class approached with a towheaded boy riding on the man's shoulders. Uncle Travis drew them into a conversation before they reached her.

Slowly Kim realized that the other adults in her family had formed a protective ring with her in the center. Apparently they'd somehow gotten the impression that she was still too fragile to deal with people.

Why would they think that unless her dad had

been talking to them about her? She stared at him, still deep in conversation. As if he could feel her gaze, he glanced over and raised his eyebrows.

She ought to be annoyed, but instead she felt as though she were standing on the prairie circled by wagons guarding against a renegade attack. Somehow she didn't figure the people here would appreciate the comparison, but the image made her want to laugh. Quickly she pressed her fingers to her lips before anyone could notice her grin and wonder about her.

"What's so funny?"

The question, muttered directly into Kim's ear, spun her around to see David lurking there. Unlike most of the men present, he was bareheaded, the bright sun bringing out the auburn streaks in his dark hair.

"You missed the service," she said. "Do you always sneak up on people or just me?" Still feeling embarrassed by her melodramatic collapse two days before, she had breathed a sigh of relief when he didn't join them earlier in the family pew.

"I got caught up in something, but I figured you'd all still be here," he replied. "Now fill me in on what you were grinning about just now, and don't try to tell me it was old Mrs. Baker's new flowered hat."

For some reason Kim found herself blurting out her impression of the Winchesters circling their wagons against their marauding neighbors. If David thought she was being ridiculous, he managed to hide it behind an attractive grin.

"Oh, yeah?" He lifted his head to glance around with a considering expression while she took the opportunity to study his profile.

He looked nothing like his mom except for his brown eyes. Kim had always thought they were his best feature, set beneath arching brows and framed by dark lashes as thick as a girl's. He topped six feet, and the reason he'd been able to carry her up the stairs so easily was evident in the way his shoulders filled out the white dress shirt he wore tucked into snug black jeans.

"Are you feeling better today?" he asked her.

She blinked, disconcerted that he'd turned and caught her staring, but at least she hadn't been checking out his butt as she'd been tempted to do.

"Yes, thanks. I just needed some rest."

He raised his brows skeptically as though he might wonder how someone who didn't even have a job could be so tired, but he didn't challenge her reply. Not that the state of her health was any of his business.

A burst of laughter from two couples standing nearby gave Kim the excuse to look away from David's probing stare.

"How did you scratch your face?" he asked.

Realizing that her habit of touching her scar must have drawn his attention to it, she immediately dropped her hand to her side.

"I got cut by flying glass from a broken window," she responded automatically.

Most people were too polite to mention the scar in the first place, but those who did usually accepted her explanation.

Not David, of course. He leaned closer and peered at her cheek. "You were lucky your eye wasn't injured."

"Yes, I was." Refusing to elaborate, she took a

step back, wishing that someone, anyone, would come along and interrupt them. Of course no one did.

There was a real downside to a protective circle.

"How come you missed church?" she asked bluntly. If he could be nosy, so could she. "Did you oversleep? Late date last night?"

When she'd been back before, he was seeing Joey Parker, but that was a long time ago and Kim had heard that Joey got married. Perhaps she had gotten tired of waiting for David to make a commitment, or maybe they hadn't been serious.

David hooked his thumbs into his wide black belt and stuck out his chin. "I've been doing some remodeling on my house and I guess I lost track of the time."

His comment didn't give her a clue as to whether he was seeing someone, but his love life was of no interest to her anyway.

"What are you remodeling?" She'd only been in the house once or twice and didn't remember much about it, but she was just trying to be polite.

"I'm redoing the master bath, and I put in a jetted tub."

"Really?" She managed to lace her tone with innuendo as she let her gaze slide over him. "Sounds like you've turned into quite the party animal."

If someone had threatened David with a hot branding iron, he wouldn't have admitted to Kim that his main intention in adding a bigger tub was to soak away the aches from a long winter day in the saddle chasing strays. If she wanted to picture him surrounded by women in bikinis, he wasn't about to disillusion her.

Let her think he had an active love life. Someone

in the family was bound to let it slip sooner or later that he hadn't been on a date in months. He'd look like even more of a chump if he tried to explain that his current celibacy was voluntary.

The loose circle of family members that had surrounded Kim when he first arrived was beginning to break up, as though her overprotective relatives expected David to watch out for her. The idea that he could be trusted with Adam's precious princess, even now, carried with it a certain amount of irony. At one point, Adam's overprotective attitude had nearly derailed his own romance with David's mother.

David was about to ask Kim why her husband hadn't come with her this time, but someone crashed into him from behind and distracted him.

"David, David, save me!" shrilled Cheyenne as she ducked between him and Kim.

"Hey, take it easy." He grabbed Cheyenne before she could knock Kim over. "Why don't you take your game over by the swings where there aren't so many people."

"Okay." She darted a subdued look at both of them. "Sorry."

"That's okay," David admonished her gently. "Just be a little more careful."

Kim remained silent until after Cheyenne had run off again. "She's gotten so big, and so has Jake," she murmured. "Your mom sent pictures, but I still wouldn't have recognized either of them."

"Kids grow in five years," David replied dryly. As soon as the words were out, he wanted to suck them back in.

Kim's expression grew mocking, and she cocked her head to the side. "Been keeping track?"

"No," he snapped, annoyed with himself. "But I'll bet Adam has." Although the older man had never shared his feelings, at least not with David, he must have been devastated by her choice to go and live with the mother who had walked out on both of them. What a slap in the face that had to be to the father who had raised her by himself.

Now Kim's eyes flashed with the first spark of real emotion David had noticed since she'd come home. "You don't know anything, so don't judge me."

Anger surged through him and he leaned closer, gratified when her eyes widened. "I wouldn't waste my time."

Leaving her gaping, he turned on his boot heel. He didn't want their exchange to turn into a full-blown argument. Before he could stalk away, his mother touched his arm, her concerned expression making him wonder how much she might have overheard.

"We're leaving now," she said with a glance over at Adam, who glared back. "Iron man needs to rest his leg. We're all getting together for dinner at our house later. You're coming, aren't you?"

David shot a look at Kim, who was studiously ignoring him as she examined her nails. Knowing she didn't want him around, and feeling perverse, he grinned back at his mom. Making her happy and annoying Kim at the same time was too good an opportunity to pass up.

"I wouldn't miss it. What can I bring?"

Kim couldn't help but overhear his reply. She had been hoping he would be too busy ripping up his house to accept, but of course he considered himself one of the family now. After his last dig about how long Kim had been away, it was clear he figured he had more right to be here than she did.

He was probably correct. One bad choice had led to another and then another, until she'd ended up feeling trapped and powerless. She wasn't about to tell David, who obviously had no use for her, how much she had longed to come back sooner.

About six months after she'd first left, if her mother hadn't begged her so hard to stay with her. And if Kim's father hadn't already been married to David's mother by then.

Chapter Three

A burst of masculine laughter from the back deck and children's shouts from the yard blended with the familiar sounds of women's chatter, drawing Kim reluctantly to her stepmother's large kitchen. After church Kim had changed out of the rose-pink dress into her usual uniform of khaki pants and long-sleeved shirt. This one was light blue with thin white stripes. In deference to the heat of the afternoon, she had rolled up the sleeves and left the top button undone.

The women of the Winchester dynasty were of course grouped in the kitchen, setting out the food. The men were outside supervising their progeny, Kim's siblings and cousins.

Feeling like the star attraction or, more likely, the star witness, and braced to field a slew of questions, she sucked in a deep breath, licked her dry lips and stepped into the arched doorway.

Predictably, all conversation died as her uncles' wives stared. Emily was the first to greet her, followed by statuesque Aunt Rory of the blazing red hair, the green thumb and the angelic voice, then Aunt Robin, a diminutive and dark-haired veterinarian from Chicago. For the first time, Kim realized that all three Winchester brothers had chosen brides from other states.

Kim waited for the inevitable questions: Why are you home? Where's your husband? How long are you staying? When are you going to start a family of your own?

Aunt Rory, the mail-order bride from the Bronx who had come out to see Uncle Charlie and married Uncle Travis instead, came forward with a big smile and open arms.

"Hi, sweetie. Welcome back."

"Thank you," Kim murmured, taking comfort in Aunt Rory's enveloping embrace and the familiar scent of her perfume. As a teenager, Kim had spent many hours baby-sitting Rory's kids.

After a final squeeze, Rory released her so she could greet Robin, the aunt she barely knew. While Rory's height dwarfed her, Robin made Kim feel oversize and gangly.

"It's nice to see you again," Robin said. Her midnight-black hair was cut as short as Kim's and her smile was a little shy.

"Thanks," Kim replied, feeling awkward. "Where's Amanda?"

At the mention of her baby, Robin's elfin face

brightened. "Charlie's got her. He hardly lets her out of his sight."

"Well, he's always been a bit of a ladies' man," Rory reminded her with a wink.

"Listen to you," Emily exclaimed, waving hands that were encased in flowered oven mitts. "As if Travis hasn't taken to fatherhood like a kitten to cream."

"Winchester men," Rory replied with a grin. "You gotta love 'em."

Watching the interplay between the other three women, all friends and all happily married, stirred a mixed brew of feelings in Kim—envy, resentment and a dash of self-pity. It wasn't fair. She had tried so hard to do everything right, so why had it all turned out so badly?

Dismissing the silent question, she turned to the woman she had blamed for a long time for usurping her own place in her father's life and heart.

"Anything I can do to help?" Kim asked.

The counter was lined with bowls of salads—pasta, potato, mixed greens and shimmery jello for the kids. Next to a large platter of fried chicken on the center island was a bowl of baked beans.

"Everything's ready, so you could start carrying the dishes outside," Emily replied with a sweep of one hand. "Rory, would you tell your hubby to get the kids settled? Robin, why don't you help Kim with the food?"

"And just what are you going to be doing while we're all slaving away?" Rory returned with a mock glare.

She had married Travis when Kim was ten, an alien goddess from New York who worked briefly as the bunkhouse cook. Now she sang at Charlie's dinner club in town when she wasn't raising children and flowers.

Robin had moved to Waterloo and married Uncle Charlie five years ago. She seemed to be as quiet as he was outgoing. Maybe opposites did sometimes mesh, rather than grinding against each other until only one was left whole.

Pushing her blond hair off her forehead, Emily made a sweeping gesture toward the open French doors. "I think I'll go mingle with all that prime male Winchester beef waiting outside." She added a shimmy of her hips for emphasis.

"In that case, dab some salad dressing behind your ears and take this with you," Rory drawled, thrusting a bowl of greens at her as the others hooted with laughter. Even Kim had to grin at their antics.

"Jake, quit picking on Chuckie!" Adam called out as David dug a cold soda from the cooler.

As Jake looked up at his father, his chubby redheaded cousin took the opportunity to push him.

"Hey!" Travis shouted at his younger son. "Any more of that and you're benched." He grinned over at his own older brother. "Tough little suckers. Probably future football stars." He looked back at the two boys, who were now both scowling fiercely. "Play nice."

"Yeah, like your dads never did," Charlie added with a sly wink at David. Charlie was holding his two-month-old baby in the crook of his arm. Oblivious to the sounds around her, Amanda slept soundly.

Even though David wasn't really into babies, she was pretty cute with her tiny fist tucked under her pointy chin. It was plain to see that his uncle, the former sheriff, was a cream puff when it came to his firstborn.

"When are you going to tie the knot and raise a passel of little Winchesters?" Travis asked him jokingly.

"He's not a Winchester!"

The heads of all four men seated around the picnic table swiveled to look at Kim, who was standing in the doorway with a platter of chicken. David couldn't tell if the color on her cheeks was caused by annoyance or merely embarrassment from suddenly finding herself the center of attention.

David got to his feet as Adam broke the awkward silence.

"But David is family just the same," he said firmly, his gaze steady on his daughter's.

Kim's knuckles were nearly as white as the platter she gripped so tightly. Somehow that tiny bit of vulnerability spurred David forward, that and the memory of a younger, gentler Kim pushing through a crowd of students to ask his name.

"Let me help you with that," he offered, reaching for the platter. "It's got to be heavy."

Her gaze clashed with his and he thought she was going to refuse.

"Rory makes the best fried chicken in the state," he added. "I'd eat it off the floor if I had to, but I'd sooner not."

"Oh, Lord, don't drop my wife's chicken, Kimmie, or I'll never hear the end of it!" Travis exclaimed dramatically. "Somebody set that plate down."

His comment broke the tension. Kim blinked and

then she thrust the platter at David. When their hands touched, he could feel her tremble.

"Thanks." Her voice was husky. "I didn't mean anything by what I said. I was just stating a fact."

"No problem," David replied. Adam didn't deserve whatever resentment she felt, but that was for the two of them to work out. David had no intention of getting in the middle.

Kim flapped her hand in the direction of the kitchen. "There are some more things I need to get." She turned abruptly, barely avoiding a collision with Rory, who was bringing the potato salad.

"Hey, kid, would you make yourself useful and help me move the tables?" Charlie asked, distracting him.

Adam reached for Amanda, his normally stern expression replaced by a goofy grin as he cuddled her. Like the Pied Piper, Travis had already led the other kids inside the house to wash up.

"What do you think is going on with Kim?" Charlie asked David after the two of them had put two tables together. "She sure seems tense."

Charlie grabbed his beer. His observation didn't surprise David as much as it might have if it had come from some other big macho guy. When he had served his term as the town sheriff, he would have had to be able to read people and to be observant. Not much got past him. David remembered that a few of his buddies had found that out the hard way.

He wasn't about to admit that he'd even given Kim a thought. He no longer had any idea of what made her tick, and perhaps he never had.

"Who knows," he replied carelessly. "Maybe it's jet lag."

"It's a three-hour flight from Seattle," Charlie pointed out dryly. "You'd think she would have recovered by now."

David shrugged. The aroma from the chicken was making his stomach growl as more food was brought out to a long side table. "Have you met the missing husband? I never did."

"Yeah, I have." Charlie took a drink of his beer. "First time at the wedding, and once when I flew out to Seattle with Adam to surprise Kim."

"Yeah?" David prompted, curious despite himself about what kind of man had managed to win her heart, and her hand.

"Piece of work," Charlie said flatly. "Ritzy wedding and a reception straight out of the movies. Food, music, booze. More attendants than a president's funeral and flowers everywhere. I heard the old man telling someone they'd flown the orchids in from Holland, and the roses from South America."

He chuckled, making David shift impatiently. It wasn't the wedding he was curious about, it was the marriage.

"When they released the white doves outside the church, I was braced for a shotgun blast," Charlie added with a grin.

"What's he like?" David asked.

"Good-looking, I guess, but cold." Charlie looked over at Kim, who had come out with a pitcher of juice for the kids and a stack of cups. "She seemed happy at the time. I s'pose most brides are on their big day, Lord knows Robin was. But now, with Kimmie, I don't know."

"What about Christie?" David asked. "Are she and Kim still close?" Kim had first gone to live with her mother in Denver, but he'd been stunned when she moved with Christie to the Northwest.

"Didn't you hear?" Charlie's brows waggled in surprise. "That gold-digging witch finally managed to .bag herself a rich, decrepit old husband. They moved to Italy not too long ago."

"Huh. I didn't know that." David wondered if Kim resented her mother's remarriage as much as she had Adam's. At least *Adam* hadn't left the country afterward.

Everyone was beginning to gather, drawn by the food like ants to a picnic. David's mother clapped her hands together. "Okay, everyone," she said briskly. "You all know the drill. Food's on, so let's eat."

After Kim had gone through the buffet line, she carried her plate to an empty place at the end of one table, right after her father, David and Emily sat down at the other with some of the kids. Kim wasn't avoiding them, not really, but someone was bound to start asking her questions she didn't feel like answering today.

Robin sat down across from Kim and glanced at her plate. "Is that what you're having?"

Kim hadn't even realized that all she had selected was green salad, jello and a few olives. "I'm just getting started," she replied, feeling defensive.

"I'm sorry." Robin looked remorseful as she unfolded a gingham checked napkin. "I'm the last one to grill you about what you're eating." She indicated her own loaded plate with a jab of her fork. "I'm still trying to lose weight from my pregnancy, but today I'm splurging."

For a few moments they talked about babies and dieting. Robin was short but more curvaceous than she had been at her wedding to Charlie.

"Are you back to work yet?" Kim asked to fill the lull before Robin could ask her anything.

Robin was a veterinarian, specializing in large animals despite her diminutive size. Kim remembered that she had first come to town at the same time someone was poisoning Winchester cattle. It turned out that a huge corporation had hired a couple of thugs to help persuade her dad and uncles to sell them the ranch. Charlie had gotten shot during the chase and subsequent arrest, but not seriously. The corporation had paid a large settlement, but Kim didn't know the details.

"I'm only working at the clinic part-time so far," Robin replied after she'd swallowed a bite of potato salad. "Doc Harmon was nice enough to wait to retire until after I had Amanda, and we've hired two more vets. So far they're working out pretty well."

"Are they both straight out of school?" Kim asked, pushing around the food on her plate. Who else would come here, besides Winchester brides and greenhorn veterinarians looking for experience?

"Todd's a young guy, but great with animals," Robin replied. "Sophie is older. She went back to school after her divorce." To Kim's surprise, Robin blinked away sudden tears.

Kim nibbled on an olive while she waited for her aunt to compose herself.

"Sorry," Robin said with a sniff. "I'm just so proud of Sophie."

"So you two have gotten to be pretty good friends?" Kim asked.

Robin nodded. "I don't know if you heard from anyone in the family, but I've been going to a support group over in Elizabeth for a few years now."

Kim shook her head, curious and yet reluctant to pry. Especially since she wasn't willing to reciprocate.

"When Sophie joined the group, she had just bailed out of a horrible marriage," Robin continued. "She had left with nothing. She was living with her kids in a shelter."

"That's awful," Kim said. She felt bad for women who were so desperate that they had nowhere else to go, especially when there were children involved. It had to be heart-wrenching to see your children going through that and know it was because of choices that you made. "Sophie must be a very determined woman."

Robin broke a piece off her roll, staring at it thoughtfully for a moment. "Not when I first met her. She had no self-confidence, no self-esteem and no fight left in her. It can't have been easy, but she's come a long way."

"That's great." Kim was beginning to feel a little uncomfortable that Robin was telling her so much about someone else's life.

Rory, who was sitting next to Robin, must have been listening, even though she had been talking to a couple of the kids. Perhaps Rory already knew Sophie's story.

Robin touched Kim's hand, distracting her. "I'm not just passing on idle gossip," she said quietly. "I would never break a confidence that way, but Sophie is proud of her accomplishments and so am I."

Kim nodded, not sure what Robin expected her to

say. "So your support group is mostly social, a group of friends?" she asked.

Now Robin's smile was rueful. "I wish." She glanced at Rory, who surprised Kim by giving her sister-in-law an encouraging nod. "I started going to the group after I got involved with your uncle," Robin said. She glanced over at Charlie, her face softening. He was deep in conversation with Steve and his sister.

"You see," Robin told Kim quietly, "I had been raped by a date back in college, but I never really dealt with it before I started seeing Charlie. I'd shut myself off, but he's a very persistent man."

"Some would say stubborn," Rory drawled.

"They're entitled to their opinions," Robin replied. She turned her attention back to Kim, who was still trying to deal with the way Robin had said the word *raped,* as calmly as if she were talking about being involved in a minor traffic accident. "Since he was the sheriff, Charlie knew about the group. After I told him what had happened to me, he encouraged me to go. He wouldn't give up until I did."

"I'm sorry." Kim wasn't sure how to respond. "That's awful." Her comment was so inadequate that she bit her lip. Having someone you went out with force himself on you must be a hundred times worse than just having your husband demand sex when you weren't in the mood, even if he did lose his temper when you tried refusing.

She started to touch her cheekbone, but then she stopped herself.

Robin waved her hand dismissively. "It's okay. It was a long time ago, and your family has been wonderful in helping me to deal with it."

So everyone *knew?* Kim couldn't imagine telling everyone about something so personal, so devastating.

"Do you ever go back over it and wonder what you could have done differently?" she blurted without thinking.

"Of course I have," Robin replied calmly. "I must have played back a thousand times in my mind everything that happened. For a long time I blamed myself."

"But it wasn't your fault," Kim protested. "You didn't ask for it."

"Of course not. No one ever deserves to be raped." Robin took another bite of potato salad, as though they'd been discussing the weather.

"Sometimes a woman just flat-out makes a dumb decision about something, and then she's got no one else to blame if it ends up a disaster," Kim mused without thinking.

Robin glanced at Kim's plate and the food she'd barely touched. Her expression was compassionate. "Don't be too hard on yourself. Sometimes all we can do is learn from our mistakes and move on."

"That's what I'm trying to do," Kim admitted, "but even though my divorce was my idea, moving on afterward is hard."

As soon as the words were out, she covered her mouth with her hand and wished she could stuff them back inside. The decree had only been final for a couple of weeks, but she hadn't meant to make a general announcement until after she had a chance to talk to her father.

"You're divorced? Why didn't you tell me?"

Even though she'd been talking quietly, she hadn't

heard the sound of his crutches clumping up behind her. From the surprised expressions around her, her father's comment had been overheard. Embarrassed, Kim ducked her head and stared at her plate.

Hers certainly wasn't the first divorce in the history of the mighty Winchester dynasty. Her parents had split up, as had David's. Aunt Rory had been married before she came out here from New York, but she, too, appeared stunned by the news of Kim's divorce.

Embarrassed, Kim stuck her bare left hand above her head, waggling her fingers for everyone to see.

"Okay," she cried out, knowing she wasn't being entirely fair, but past caring. "For anyone who missed my father's big announcement, yes, I'm divorced, okay? Any other personal questions I can answer while we're on the subject?"

"I didn't realize you were having problems." Aunt Rory's voice was low as she leaned closer. "Honey, are you holding up okay?"

Kim bobbed her head, feeling immediately ashamed of her outburst.

"What can we do to help?" Aunt Robin asked.

Her aunts' sympathetic smiles and her father's firm hand on her shoulder were almost more than Kim could deal with. She looked around, her gaze meeting Emily's.

Afraid she would cry and humiliate herself further, Kim shot to her feet, bumping into her father so that he staggered before he caught himself.

"I'll be right back," she mumbled.

"What's wrong with Kim?" she heard one of the kids demand in a piercing voice as she fled through the French doors.

Feeling like a fool, Kim kept her head down as she walked quickly toward the powder room. She wished she could hide out for a while, but where would she go? She was staying here at the house, and she didn't even have a car.

Blinking away tears, she turned the corner of the hallway and barreled into David, who was coming from the opposite direction. Colliding with his chest felt like slamming into a concrete wall.

"Whoa!" He gripped her upper arms to steady her. "Where's the fire, princess?"

One second David had been walking down the hall, minding his own business and looking forward to his mom's chocolate layer cake, then the next instant he was nearly taken out by a human dynamo.

Kim twisted out of his grip. He was about to say something sarcastic about people who didn't watch where they were going when he saw the tear tracks on her cheeks. Like most rough, tough cowboy types, he wasn't scared of much, but flash floods and crying women probably topped the list.

"What's wrong?" he asked as he looked down at her bowed head. Even hacked boyishly short, the strands of her hair caught the light like threads of silk.

"Nothing! I'm fine."

He grabbed at her reply with the same sense of relief he might a life ring that had been tossed to him in a rip tide. He had done his duty, now it was on to dessert before the cake was gone.

"Good. Okay, whatever." He backed quickly away. Ignoring him, she bolted into the powder room and slammed the door. An instant later he heard water running.

David was eager to get back outside to the company of people who weren't showing awkward emotions or having embarrassing meltdowns. Kim had told him she was okay and she could have asked for his help if she wanted it. Besides, no one had ever died from crying, not as far as he knew. So how much more reassurance did he need before he could make himself walk away?

The silent argument he was conducting with himself wasn't working. His feet stayed rooted in place, refusing to move. Knowing that his stepsister, his former best friend and love of his life was in some kind of distress, his conscience just plain wouldn't allow him to leave.

He pressed his ear to the solid wood of the powder room door, hoping like hell that no one else was about to come along and ask just what he thought he was doing. All he could hear from inside was the sound of the faucet.

"Kim?"

"Go away." Her voice was muffled, as though she had a towel pressed to her face.

He sighed. "You okay?" he asked again.

"Yeah, sure thing." Her voice had risen. "Beat it, Boy Scout."

Ouch. He could hear the irritation in her tone. Normally it might make him smile, since annoying his stepsister was not intrinsically a bad thing.

Except when she was crying as though her heart had been broken. Damn.

He reached for the brass knob, thought better of it

and tapped lightly on the door with his knuckles instead.

"There's another john in the mud room, as you very well know," she called out. "Go away!"

David turned at the distinctive sound of Adam's crutches on the hardwood floor. With him was David's mother, both of them looking concerned. She pointed at the closed powder room door, her eyebrows raised in silent query.

David was tempted, really tempted, to let the two of them take over. Instead he walked over to them.

"What's up with her?" he asked, jerking his thumb in the direction of the powder room.

"Did you know about Kim's divorce?" Adam demanded in a harsh whisper.

Shock slapped at David like a wave of cold water. No wonder she looked so beat up. "She never said a thing to me," he replied. "I swear. When did she tell you?"

"It came out just now." His mother glanced at the closed door. "Is she pretty upset?"

Giving in to his curiosity over Kim's waterworks and the sense of duty that he hadn't quite been able to shake, he tapped his own chest to indicate that he had the situation under control.

What a laugh.

"She'll be okay," he said. "Let me talk to her."

A muscle flexed in Adam's jaw and then his shoulders drooped. "Yeah, thanks."

After David's mother sent him a smile of encouragement and a thumbs-up, she followed quietly after her husband, one slim hand resting on his back in a gesture of comfort David suspected would do little good. Once they were both out of sight, he folded his arms and leaned his shoulder against the wall.

"I'm not leaving until I know you're okay," he told Kim through the closed door.

After a moment the sound of running water stopped. "I'm fine."

"I want to see for myself," he insisted.

"What is it, padre? Do you need a visual before you're willing to give me your blessing and leave me in peace? Or are you waiting for some lurid confession?"

For a split second, he was tempted to ram his shoulder against the door and force it open. The gesture might go a long way toward venting his frustration, but it probably wasn't what Kim needed right now.

David leaned back his head, teeth clenched. Obviously the news of Kim's divorce had been as big a surprise to Adam and the rest of the family as it was to him.

What had happened to derail her storybook romance, and why hadn't she said anything earlier? Was it because she still carried a torch for her ex?

The door opened a crack, just wide enough for him to see one green eye and a sliver of her face through the opening.

"Good enough?" she demanded, her tone laced with sarcasm.

It would take a real idiot to wrap his fingers around the edge of the door so she could shut it and smash them, but David wasn't an idiot.

"Come on out," he coaxed instead. "Let's talk."

"Why?" At least she didn't slam the door shut again.

He shrugged, thinking fast. "What could it hurt? I'll snag us a couple of cold sodas and we can walk down to the stables." Maybe his mother would put a piece of that cake aside for him if he asked her nicely.

No, not there, Kim thought in response to his suggestion, ducking behind the door. She hadn't been inside the stable since she had walked in on her father with Emily ten years ago, but neither was she ready to parade herself back outside. Not after her melodramatic exit.

"Could we walk down toward the bunkhouse?" Her voice sounded small even to her own ears.

Still asking some man's permission, still braced for his scorn. Old habits, and those that weren't so old, died hard.

"Sure thing." David's voice sounded falsely hearty. "Do you want a soda?"

"Just water, I guess." Leaning against the door, she listened to his departing footsteps and wondered why he was bothering to befriend her after the way she had treated him in the past, leaving without saying goodbye. It had been a long time ago, so perhaps it didn't matter to him anymore. Or maybe their importance to each other had merely been a figment of her own mind all along.

She took a quick peek in the powder room mirror and saw that she looked about as bad as she'd feared, her eyes puffy and her skin all splotchy. She considered for about a nanosecond running upstairs to apply lip gloss and a spritz of cologne, then snapped back to reality. Toward the end of her marriage she had stopped primping for her husband, so she sure as heck wasn't going to start doing so for her step-brother.

When she came out of the bathroom, she heard his voice from outside, probably explaining to everyone that the loony needed fresh air and someone to keep an eye on her. Fingers laced tightly together, she wished she had gone straight upstairs when she had the chance and locked herself in her room. Too late now. Here he came with a bottle of water in one hand and a beer in the other, a baseball cap on his head and a somber expression that reminded her suddenly of the first time she had seen him.

Kim was standing with a knot of freshman girls in the hallway of the ancient high school. It was the morning break and they were all admiring Heather's new skirt when Jen suddenly stopped working her gum and stared slack-jawed at something beyond Kim's shoulder.

"Holy cow!" Jen squealed. "Where did *he* come from?"

The busy hallway went silent as every student, Kim included, immediately swiveled around to stare at a boy with spiked hair in a shade of orange Kim was willing to bet was no more a product of nature than the vice principal's teeth. The boy was wearing a blue shirt made of some shiny fabric over black slacks with a satin stripe running down the outside, like the pants to a tuxedo.

"Omygod! Is that an earring?" Heather whispered loudly.

All of the girls giggled except for Kim. She wanted to see the boy's face, but his head was bowed over a piece of paper in his hand, as though he had no clue that everyone had stopped to gawk.

"Look at the moron! Hey, where's your red nose, Bozo?" The speaker was Lenny Gordon, the school bully, star football player and number-one jerk. Too bad Kim's opinion about him wasn't shared by more of the students.

The stranger's head finally came up as though he had just realized he was the center of attention. As his face turned red, Lenny elbowed one of his posse of·goons, all wearing matching WHS lettermen's jackets.

Of course they laughed. How totally lame!

The new boy held up the piece of light-green paper he'd been studying, and Kim recognized it as a class schedule. That meant he was enrolled here. He was also, despite the bizarre hair and weird clothes, really cute.

"Can anyone point me toward the library?" he asked.

A fresh wave of giggles broke out among Kim's friends, whose immaturity mortified her.

"Yeah, sure," Lenny drawled. His sudden helpfulness was a surprise, but then he pointed in the opposite direction from the library, which was down on the main floor. "Go all the way to the end of the hall and straight through the double doors on your left."

Lenny had just directed him straight to the girls' rest room. The sign had fallen off the door the week before, but the maintenance man, who had to be a hundred years old, hadn't put it back up yet.

"Thanks, man," the new boy said with the briefest flicker of an answering smile.

"No problem." Lenny snickered. His posse was laughing and snorting so hard that a couple of them were bent over double, clutching their guts.

As the warning bell rang, Kim glanced around to see if anyone else was going to speak up. She had known most of them all her life and many of them were her friends, but right now she was totally disappointed.

As if she realized Kim's intention, Jen grabbed her arm and shook her head. "Don't say anything," she hissed.

No one ever stood up to Lenny.

The new boy was already walking away when Kim hurried after him.

"Hey, Kim!"

She ignored the warning tone in Lenny's voice. She didn't care that he thought he was God's gift to the female side of the student body.

"Um, excuse me," she called out instead. "Excuse me. Wait up."

The crowd of kids parted like the Red Sea in that movie with the really lame special effects. Finally the boy stopped and turned. He had pretty brown eyes. Wearing the right clothes, with a normal haircut, he would be a total babe.

"I'm Kim." Her heart was banging like a bongo drum, but she didn't figure her sudden breathlessness had anything to do with hurrying after him.

The sides of his head were shaved! Maybe he'd been sick or had some kind of operation.

"I'm going to the library," she added with a sympathetic smile. "I can show you where it is, if you want. What's your name?"

* * *

Funny, in a way it didn't seem like it had been so long ago, but at other times she felt as though she had lived a lifetime since that spring.

"Ready?" David asked as he handed her the bottle of cold water.

"I guess." Suddenly she was thirsty. "Thanks for the water."

"Sure thing." His fingers curled under her elbow. This time she managed, just barely, to stop herself from jerking away. Instead she just stepped ahead of him and went down the hall to the front door, leaving him to follow or not, whichever he chose.

And telling herself, as she tipped back her head and let some of the cool water trickle down her throat, that she didn't care either way.

Chapter Four

David walked with Kim along the road leading to the bunkhouse and some of the other outbuildings. High clouds had drifted in, pushed along by a cooling breeze. In a few months being outdoors would become a misery, but today it was a treat. The depth of his feelings for this country wasn't something David dwelled on, but sometimes it amazed him. He might not be a rancher by birth or blood, but he was certainly one by choice. There was nothing else he wanted to do, nowhere else he would rather be.

He filled his lungs with the clean, dry air. "I love Colorado at this time of year," he said expansively as he glanced at Kim's profile.

"Why?" Her head was bowed as she picked her way carefully along the dirt road. "It's dusty and everything is dried out."

She stumbled on a pebble, but she recovered without his assistance. Back in school she had always seemed to vibrate with energy, always wanting to go and see and do. Questioning. Laughing. She never sat still or remained quiet for more than a few seconds at a time, reminding him of a butterfly. He'd found her enthusiasm attractive and infectious.

Now tension radiated from her like heat rising from an asphalt parking lot. Her arms were wrapped tightly around her waist as if to keep her from flying apart.

He thought about her divorce and answered her question instead. "Because the sun feels good and it's not time yet to start the last cut on the haying or think about the roundup or beef prices, I guess." He tipped his head back, the better to feel the sun's rays on his face. "Does it really rain all the time in Seattle, or is that just a rumor?"

She snorted. "That's what we tell people from California so they won't all move north."

He noticed that she said we, as though she belonged there. A transplant, just like him.

"The summers are nice," she continued. "Warm and sunny, but there's always a breeze off the water. Lots of rain in the winter, but not much snow, which I don't miss."

"You like it there," he ventured.

"It's all right." She shrugged, a quick jerk of her shoulders. "Why don't you ask me what you really want to know?"

"What's that?" He was hedging and they both knew it. Impatience flashed across her face. He hadn't fooled her.

"About my divorce."

He took a long pull on the beer he'd brought with

him while he debated pointing out that her life wasn't
the center of his universe.

"How long has it been?" he asked.

Her chin went up, her smile as brittle as pond ice
in the spring as she held up her fingers and ticked
off the numbers.

"Four months since he first moved out, over three
since I filed. Two weeks since it was final, over,
ended, kaput." She stuck out her arms, leaned back
her head and turned in a circle like a little kid, right
in the middle of the road. "I'm a free woman."

"So hubby left you?" he asked. Had the jerk
found a new playmate?

"No!" she said. "I kicked him out, and the divorce was my idea."

Was she nursing a broken heart, or was that anger
he saw in her eyes?

"I'm sorry things didn't work out." His words and
tone sounded stuffy to his own ears.

Her head was turned away. "Thanks."

They came to the *Y* in the road. One branch went
to the main gate and the other past some of the buildings, including the bunkhouse. He was afraid she'd
want to go back, but she didn't say anything as they
walked past some of the horses from the working
string grazing in the field.

What they lacked in looks, with their jug heads
and broom tails, they more than made up for in cow
sense. The ranch hands spent plenty of time in the
saddle when wheeled vehicles wouldn't do the job,
but Adam had given most of them this weekend off.
A rider who'd drawn a short straw stirred up a distant
cloud of dust as he rode fence, checking for breaks.

Had Kim missed the ranch while she was away,

or had she become part of Seattle's local country club and tennis set? Or the club scene even David had heard about.

"What went wrong?" he asked, finally caving in to his curiosity.

She fiddled with the stopper on her water bottle. "I wish I knew."

As she tipped back her head and swallowed, he watched the delicate muscles working in her throat. His own mouth went dry. She had changed, but she was still so pretty that she made him ache. At least he wasn't lusting after a married woman.

They walked for a few minutes in silence, side by side, and he didn't think she was going to add anything more. Maybe all she needed was a little air, a break from being scrutinized by their big, noisy family.

Was she used to a busy social life with her hubby's attorney friends in Seattle? Did they spend time together hiking or kayaking or clamming on the miles of beaches? Or did Drew go one way and she another, as many couples did?

David had no clue and refused to ask. Her departure from Waterloo and from him had been like the incision by a surgeon's scalpel, quick and clean, without much blood.

Minimal scarring.

Suddenly she stopped in her tracks, biting her lip as she gazed up at him.

"What's wrong?" Alarm ripped through him. Was she tired? Feeling dizzy? He didn't want her to faint again. "Are you okay?"

She looked upset. "I never asked if you were

through eating before I dragged you out here with me. How stupid.''

He let out his breath. ''I was the one who offered, okay? Don't worry about it.'' Following an impulse, he reached for her hand. ''You saved me from helping with the dishes, so I guess I owe you.''

''You do dishes?'' she asked lightly, letting their joined hands swing between them. ''A big, bad cowboy?'' The corners of her full mouth turned up, a sharp reminder of the attraction that had always lurked beneath their teenage friendship, at least for him.

''When the women cook, the men do KP,'' he replied, struggling to stay focused. ''It's a Winchester tradition.'' He drained his beer, even though it had grown too warm for his taste, and crushed the can. He set it on a fence post so he could retrieve it on their way back to the house.

''A first-generation tradition, from what I've heard.''

''And what's wrong with being a cowboy, anyway?'' he teased. ''Chasing cattle built this ranch.''

She shrugged. ''I know that. Nothing is wrong with it as long as flies and dust are what floats your boat.''

''Not many boats floating around here,'' he pointed out. ''Not much water.''

''If it makes you happy.''

He stopped walking, still clinging tightly to her hand. ''What makes Kim happy?''

She thought for a minute, gaze wide. ''I guess I've forgotten the answer to that one.''

''Is that why you're here, to figure it out?'' For a crazy moment he wondered what he would do if she were to throw herself into his arms and confess that she had never gotten over him.

He'd been in the sun too long to be replaying that old fantasy.

"Maybe I just had nowhere else to go." Her voice was husky, her cheeks fiery pink.

He cocked his head to the side, studying her as she looked away. "That's hard to believe," he said. "You must have a life. Friends? A job?"

She laughed lightly, but it was tinged with bitterness. "Drew never wanted me to work, and my friends were the wives of his friends, his associates, his family's business connections."

"Ah. So they all took his side," David guessed.

"Pretty much." She shrugged. "My in-laws have a lot of power in Seattle, and Gloria never forgets a slight."

"Gloria?" David echoed.

"Drew's mother, a pillar of the social scene."

"Wow," David muttered. "So she'd cut anyone who stuck by you from her Christmas card list?"

Kim's lips twitched. "At the very least. She serves on a lot of committees, and she knows a lot of people. Influential people."

"People who matter," David added.

Kim nodded. "Exactly."

"Do I know any of them?" he asked.

"Who?" Her expression was puzzled.

"The people who matter."

She frowned. "Probably not. Why?"

It was his turn to shrug. "So they don't matter a lot around here."

"Probably not," she repeated. Then her expression relaxed. "It sounds kind of silly, when you put it like that."

He didn't smile. "Not when it kept your so-called friends from sticking by you."

"Well, I guess that's what family is for." She looked surprised, as though she'd just remembered that. "To answer your earlier question, I suppose that's the reason I'm here."

He squeezed her hand. "Good girl."

David led her over to a large flat rock no one had ever bothered to move. The road curved around it. They sat down and she slipped her hand free of his so she could lean back and brace herself on her arms.

A couple of butterflies hovered nearby. Kim watched them, and David watched her, willing her to look at him.

"If you need a good listener, just start at the beginning," he suggested.

"Why?" she countered. "It's the end that got interesting, the part where I kicked him out." Her finger moved unerringly to the scar on her face.

"Did he do that?" David hadn't realized that his hands had fisted in his lap until Kim glanced down. Heat flooded his face as he unclenched his fingers.

"It was flying glass, remember?" Her tone was flat, as though she were reciting a programmed response, but a mocking smile curved her lips—either inviting David to share the joke or asking him to accept the only answer she was capable of giving. He couldn't tell which.

He forced aside his feeling of helplessness. "I could go beat him up." Deliberately, he made his tone light.

She cocked her head to the side, considering. "You'd do that for me?"

The question hung in the air between them like a bright, colorful balloon.

"Damn right I would." The words came out way too husky. "What are friends for?" he added, scrambling to save face.

To his astonishment, she leaned over and kissed his cheek. "I never deserved a friend like you," she whispered, straightening back up. "I still don't."

"You're wrong." His voice was hoarse, his chest tight. His gaze slid to her mouth. He could still feel the featherlight touch of it against his skin. The friendly peck hadn't been nearly enough, not for him.

The sound of an approaching Jeep reminded him that they were sitting alongside the road, visible from all directions. Only a worn-out muffler had prevented his personal humiliation, as well as the probability that she would have become the butt of bunkhouse gossip. He settled for tapping her chin with his finger as the Jeep took the other fork in the road.

"It will be okay."

"Of course it will." Kim got to her feet, looking everywhere except at him. "I'm still a Winchester, since my in-laws requested that I not keep their name."

She'd nearly made a pass at her stepbrother, in broad daylight and full view of anyone caring to look! If not for the sound of the Jeep engine, she might have followed her sisterly peck on the cheek with something more.

Poor David. He'd offered to be her friend, not her shrink and certainly not her boy toy.

As they walked back to the house, three feet separating them, she tried desperately to think of something to break the silence.

"How about those Broncos." His voice startled her.

Kim stared, openmouthed, as he looked straight ahead. Then the absurdity of his comment hit her and she began to laugh helplessly. Grinning, he joined her. They were still both chuckling when they walked up the driveway.

The first thing Kim noticed was her father seated on the bench by the front door. From there, the big rock was easily visible.

Had he been spying on them the entire time?

"Guess I'm getting old," he said when they reached the steps. "I was looking for a little peace and quiet." From the backyard, the sounds of children playing was audible but not deafening. "Did you go for a walk?" he asked, his face a picture of weathered innocence.

"We wanted some air," David replied in an easy voice.

Once again, Kim found herself feeling envious of his close relationship with her father.

"How's your leg?" she asked. She had heard Emily worrying out loud about him before they all ate. It sounded as though he hadn't changed all that much when it came to being hardheaded.

"It's good." He slapped his thigh for emphasis and then jerked a thumb at the crutches leaning by the door. "I'll be able to do away with those tomorrow."

"If the doctor agrees," David reminded him. He

was carrying the crushed beer can and her water bottle.

Adam grinned up at him. "Of course."

Kim stepped closer, needing to regain her father's attention. "Can I get you anything, Daddy?"

He barely glanced at her. "No thanks, honey. If David has the time, I want to go over tomorrow's schedule with him."

His gaze shifted, dismissing her. Demeaning her. It was an unnecessary reminder that she was no longer his princess. "Whatever," she mumbled.

David was frowning when he glanced back and forth between them. "Can it wait awhile?" he asked Adam.

"Oh, please. Don't postpone your meeting on my account," Kim blurted, embarrassed that he would feel the need to stick up for her with her own parent. "I'm a little tired, so I thought I'd take a nap."

Her father finally focused his attention on her. "Good idea. You look pretty worn-out," he said tactlessly. He probably couldn't wait for her to leave so they could discuss *men's* work.

"I'll see you later," David said, touching the bill of his cap as though it were a Stetson.

"Thanks for, um, everything," she replied. From the corner of her eye, she could see that her father was watching the two of them closely, his scrutiny making her feel self-conscious. Perhaps he was recalling how she had flirted with David the summer he started working at the ranch, and his own scowling disapproval.

She pushed her way through the double front doors into the house and took a deep breath. She could still hear the voices and laughter coming from the patio, but the noise didn't matter. Even though her bedroom overlooked the backyard, she wasn't really tired.

She had been incredibly rude earlier when she had bolted from her own unofficial welcoming party. She might as well put in a quick appearance, thank Emily for arranging it, and let them all know she hadn't had a meltdown, at least not yet.

"How do you think she's doing?" Adam drummed his fingers on his knee. He looked tired.

"Okay, I guess." David wasn't sure how much to say. "Have you had a chance to talk with her since she came back?"

"Not really." Adam's voice cooled and he looked away.

David knew the signs. When Adam didn't want to discuss something, he put up barriers that only his wife had the guts to ignore. David took a leaf from her book and waited, feigning patience.

"Hearing about her divorce was quite a shock," Adam volunteered after a few moments had passed.

"I can imagine. She didn't give any indication they were having problems before this?" David probed.

A muscle flexed in Adam's jaw. "She doesn't confide in me."

"Well, she's probably got girlfriends she tells *everything,*" David suggested, rolling his eyes. If he was shocked to hear that she'd split from her husband, think how her father must feel.

Adam nodded. "I hope so. It sounds as though her own mother bailed on her again, just when Kim may have needed her support."

David's father and Kim's mother were a matched

set, neither likely to get nominated for a parent-of-the-year award anytime soon. Christie hadn't bothered to stay in touch with Kim for the first fifteen years of her life, and his father had abandoned both David and his mother for newer, younger models, a new wife and a new son. David was an adult, past caring, but he felt sorry for his half brother, Zane, who was only ten, now that their father had moved on yet again.

He should call Zane sometime and see how the kid was doing.

"Why do you suppose Kim went with Christie when she moved from Denver to Seattle?" he asked Adam without thinking.

Adam's expression closed up as abruptly as a steel bear trap. "I reckon that's something you'd have to ask Kim," he said gruffly, scratching his jaw. "She sure as hell never saw fit to enlighten me."

"But you knew why she left here in the first place."

Adam glared, narrow-eyed. "Did I? Shucks, son, I was just the one who struggled to hang on to the ranch after Daddy dropped dead, keep my younger brothers in line and raise her up from a little tike to a know-it-all teenager. Why would there be any reason for her to bring me into the loop of why she up and left with the mama who walked out on her?"

For the first time David could remember hearing when Kim's name had come up, Adam's tone was bitter. "Maybe I was too strict with her, like she always said," he continued, "but I was afraid she'd run wild without a mother to guide her. I did my best. Then Christie crooked her finger and Kim bolted like a runaway filly."

''But she needed your permission,'' David argued. ''You had sole custody.''

Adam's laugh was humorless. ''Trust me, that's a mere technicality when your fifteen-year-old daughter threatens to run away if you don't agree to let her go.''

The news didn't surprise David. He had been the one to give her a ride to the bus station on his motorbike when she threatened to hitchhike if he didn't. Then he'd called his mother and Adam had shown up to drag Kim back home. David's mother had broken up with Adam for a while after that, but they had eventually gotten back together.

''I'm sorry.'' He felt bad for bringing up the subject.

Adam tipped back his head and closed his eyes. ''I ask myself if her marriage going bust is somehow my fault,'' he mumbled. ''Was I too unbending when I should have said yes, or too easy when I needed to stand firm?''

David didn't think Adam expected an answer. Before he could decide for sure, Adam cleared his throat and sat back up.

''I want you to check out the southwest hayfield in the morning,'' he said briskly. ''Let me know if the grass is ready for cutting. On your way back, see about that little cream heifer Hank mentioned had a bad-looking eye. Call the broker about the auction next month, make sure Jones got the big tractor fixed and find out what the hell is the delay on that load of fence posts I ordered. They should have been here on Tuesday.''

With a sigh, David sat down on the top step, took the small notebook he always carried from his shirt pocket and shifted around so his back rested against the corner post. Apparently Adam had said everything about his concerns for Kim that he intended. A ranch, he was fond of saying, didn't run itself, especially not one as large as the Running W.

Kim lay on her narrow bed and reread the letter from the attorney, her frustration building like steam with no release valve, until she thought she might have to either scream at the top of her lungs or blow apart like a cheap boiler. Instead she swore under her breath and tossed the single page aside.

Damn Atherton anyway! He couldn't manage one thing right, not even something as simple as retrieving the personal items Kim had left behind. That would teach her to pick a bargain-basement divorce attorney from the phone book to face the high-priced pit bull her former father-in-law had hired.

Atherton sent his regrets that Kim's things had already been "disposed of" by Drew's mother. His letter went on to warn Kim that he would have to bill her for the additional time if she wanted him to pursue the matter further.

To do what, try to find out what thrift store had been the recipient of Gloria's generosity?

They'd had no legal right, Kim fumed, but when did the legalities stop people like the Sterlings from doing what they pleased? How many times had she heard Drew say that laws meant to keep the riffraff in line didn't apply to them?

On one of their first dates, he had pulled into a handicapped spot in front of the tennis club. When she pointed it out, he told her that handicapped people had no business playing tennis. She had been shocked, of course, but she'd laughed because he expected her to and she wanted to please him.

Eventually his arrogance had stopped being amusing.

There was nothing funny about this, either, but what could she could do? Her family owned one of the largest cattle ranches in Colorado, but to her former in-laws, she was still riffraff.

Kim stared at the wall of her bedroom, papered in the same gingham and flowered print the housekeeper, Betty, had helped pick out when Kim was twelve. If she didn't get out of here, at least for a little while, she'd go crazy. She considered taking a walk, but she was too restless for that. Besides, it would be dark soon. Then she had a better idea.

Unbuttoning her shirt as she got off the bed, she pawed through the pitiful number of hangers in her closet.

David was dreaming, something about a hot tub, lots of steam and women in bikinis, when a phone started ringing. Why would he have brought his cell phone into the water with him?

Belatedly he realized he was in his bedroom alone and the ringing phone was on his nightstand. Sitting up, he cracked open his eyes against the darkness. Lulu stood next to the bed and Calvin was a lump at his feet.

The phone rang again and Lulu whined. The glowing numbers on the clock radio showed that it was after eleven, past bedtime for a rancher whose day started before dawn.

He rubbed a hand over his face and picked up the

receiver. "Yeah?" It wasn't a social call, not at this hour.

"Dave, is that you?" The voice was male, one he didn't recognize, but the loud music and laughter in the background eliminated an emergency at the ranch.

"Who's calling?" His voice was rough from sleep. Familiar shapes appeared as his eyes adjusted to the darkness.

"Uh, this is Joe Willy, the bartender down at the Longhorn. Do you remember me? We, uh, went to school together."

What the hell? "Yeah, how are you? What's up?" If Joe Willy was calling to say hello, David was going to find out where he lived and pay him a visit some morning. Just to repay the favor.

"Uh, sorry to wake you, but we've got a situation down here and I didn't know quite what to do. She threatened me with personal bodily harm if I called her father."

David blinked hard. Was he really awake, or was this just another dream? A bad one. Whichever it happened to be, he was doing a damn poor job of following the plot.

"Joe Willy, you've got thirty seconds to start making sense or I'm coming down there to the Longhorn and I promise you it won't be pretty." It was hard to sound tough around a yawn. "Now, start over. Who the hell are you talking about and why are you calling me?"

Joe Willy whispered something that David couldn't hear over the music in the background. The cat added its own complaint when David moved his foot under the covers.

"What?" he demanded, squeezing the receiver in frustration. "Speak up, man!"

Calvin jumped off the bed. Through the receiver came the sound of arguing, followed by a burst of static.

"He's got my damn car keys and he won't give them back!"

Kim! That was Kim's voice screeching through the phone straight into David's ear.

"What's going on?" Damn, but he was fully awake now. "What are you doing down at the Long-horn?"

She giggled, shocking him. "I'm socializing." She didn't sound quite sober, which shocked him even more.

"Well, I guess that technically they aren't my keys, since it's not actually my car," she added with a snort.

There were more sounds of scuffling, and then Joe Willy's voice came back on the line.

"You see the problem?" he whined. "I don't think she should drive. Should I call her father to come and fetch her, or do you just want me to get a deputy to run her up home? It probably won't be no big deal."

Charlie's replacement was a family friend, but word would get around and Adam would be furious.

David was already on his feet, reaching for the clothes he'd left on the chair.

"No! Don't call anyone else, do you hear me, and don't let her leave. I'm on my way."

Slamming down the receiver, he hopped around on one foot and then the other as he pulled on his jeans. Fifteen minutes later he walked into the Longhorn. It was the first time he'd been to the place in months, but the decor was unchanged. Neon beer signs lined the wall. Dark wood and loud music. A haze of cigarette smoke made everything appear fuzzy in the glow from dangling light fixtures shaped like western boots.

Joe Willy was behind the bar, rubbing circles into the worn surface with a rag. When he saw David, he nodded toward a table at the edge of the tiny dance floor.

A woman sat alone, shoulders slumped over a cup of coffee in front of her. Even in the dim light, he could tell it was Kim.

The band was on a break, but two couples were slow dancing to the canned music. One of the girls recognized David and blew him a wet kiss over her partner's shoulder.

He slid a folded twenty across the bar to Joe Willy. It disappeared in a blink, his free hand dipping into the pocket of his faded black jeans.

"What's been going on?" David asked him.

"Dunno. She come prancing in a couple of hours ago, all dolled up and sassy as a new silver dollar." He nodded goodbye at a customer who was leaving. "At first I just figured she was looking for a little fun, you know what I mean?"

David's stomach clenched at the thought, but his brain had snagged on "all dolled up." Kim? He hadn't seen her in lipstick since she'd come back.

Small town or not, there were drifters and tourists and strangers passing through, plus Waterloo had its own share of lowlife scum who might get the wrong idea or take advantage of a single woman who was less than sober.

"Yeah. So then what?" he prompted, one eye on Kim. She hadn't turned around, nor had she touched her coffee, that he could tell. At least none of the ragtag barflies seated on the row of stools had approached her since David walked in.

"She parked her butt at that table, prime location. She's been baring her teeth at anyone who got within biting distance." Joe Willy wiped another circle on the surface of the bar. "She hasn't had all that much to drink, just a few beers. She turned down the free ones anyone tried to send her, but when she got up and wobbled past me, I grabbed her keys and called you."

He straightened self-righteously and puffed out his skinny chest, covered by a leather vest over a stained T-shirt. "I woulda felt just terrible if she got into trouble on her way home."

David didn't bother to add that Joe Willy would have felt even worse if she hit someone and he got sued for serving her.

"Thanks. You did the right thing." David turned away. The idea of any of these creeps sending her free drinks or hitting on her set his jaw. The thought of her involved in an accident was enough to slick a cold sweat over his skin, followed by a blast of temper that boiled his blood as he walked over to her table.

Circling around so he was in her line of vision, he grabbed an empty chair and straddled it backward. The sight of her in a skimpy tank top and full makeup, eyes shadowed seductively and mouth a red flag of temptation, slammed into him like a fist. Instead of dousing his anger, her altered appearance managed to stoke it like gas on a bonfire.

Her head tipped back and her slightly bleary eyes widened as she recognized him.

"Well, if it isn't my stepbrother," she drawled, batting her lashes so hard he could damn near feel a breeze. She lifted her full coffee cup in a mocking toast and managed to slosh some of the contents onto the table between them.

"Whoops!" She slammed it back down, spilling a little more, and set her elbows on the table. "So, Davy dearest, why are you here?" Her pouty grin was totally without remorse.

"The bartender called." David tried his best to ignore the hint of cleavage revealed by the scooped-out neckline of her fire-engine-red top when she leaned toward him. The fabric molded to the shape of her breasts as faithfully as paint on a fender. Despite her weight loss, he couldn't help but notice that the twin mounds would fill his hands and her nipples looked as hard as that portion of his own anatomy he was trying desperately to ignore.

Damn! He was reacting like a green kid in a strip club, and that wasn't why he'd come down here.

"I'm not drunk," she insisted, enunciating as carefully as someone who'd been drinking always did. "I'm just, um, tipsy." She giggled, the sound sliding over David's nerves like a stroke from her hot, wet tongue. "That's it," she added with a nod of emphasis. "I'm just a li'l tipsy."

"What provoked this 'tipsiness'?" he demanded, leaning closer. Her perfume, as spicy as mulled cider, teased his nose. This was the first time she'd bothered to wear scent since her arrival, at least around him. "Do you have a problem with alcohol?"

Kim managed to look offended. "Oh, please! You

sound as stuffy as Daddy. 'A problem with alcohol?'" she mimicked. "No, I don't. I happen to have a problem with my attorney back in Seattle."

"I thought the divorce was final." If she was still married, even technically, it was one more reason for David to ignore the shape of her breasts or anything else sending his blood rushing south of his belt. Not that he needed another reason, but he had never in his life lusted after someone else's wife.

"It is." She took a sip of the coffee that had to be as cold as it was black and turned to signal the bartender, mug upraised.

"*Garçon,* if you please!" she demanded.

David stuck up two fingers. Might as well join her.

Joe Willy brought over the pot and two fresh mugs. After he'd filled them, wiped the table and left again, Kim rested her chin on her hands and massaged her temples with the tips of her long, slim fingers.

David fought the need to squirm. "Headache?" he asked with a smirk. She deserved it after dragging him down here.

Her grin was a little less artificial. "Not like the one I've been warned I'll have in the morning."

"You mean you've never been hung over before?" he demanded as she blew gently on her coffee. The sight of her puckered lips almost sent his good intentions up in smoke.

She took an experimental sip. "Nope," she replied. "I've never been drunk in my life. How about you?"

He shrugged. Back in college a couple of experiments had shown him he didn't enjoy giving up control, let alone puking and looking stupid. After that he'd nearly always been the designated driver for his bingeing buddies. "Once or twice, I guess, a long time ago."

He took a drink of his own coffee and almost spit it back out. "This is bilge!"

"Surprise, surprise, we actually agree on something." Her tone had resumed its usual bite. Maybe that meant she was sobering up.

"So tell me about your attorney," he suggested. "What happened?"

Before she could answer, the band, which had just returned from its break, jumped on a fast number with all the finesse of an elephant stomping out a fire. What they lacked in talent, they more than made up for in volume.

"Let's get out of here," David shouted. "Hungry?"

Looking alarmed, Kim pressed a hand to her stomach and shook her head. "Not really."

He made a sudden decision, ignoring the voice of reason that was waving a warning flag in a futile attempt to get his attention.

"Come on." He leaned across the table so she could hear him. "I'll take you back to my place and fix you some soup or toast. Trust me, you'll feel better for it."

She stayed seated, her expression mulish. "What about my car? I mean, the ranch car?"

"It will be okay." He took out his wallet and tossed down a couple of bills to pay for the coffee. "I'll come back in the morning, before Mom needs it."

To his horror, sudden tears filled Kim's eyes. He wasn't about to watch her break down in public, so he got to his feet and tugged on her arm. Luckily she didn't resist.

Joe Willy wished them both good-night when they left and gave David a thumbs-up and a wink behind Kim's back. The other man was probably envisioning a much different ending to David's evening than he was.

An impossible, fantasy ending that David absolutely refused to let into his conscious mind.

Chapter Five

"I'm feeling a lot better now," Kim argued as David pulled up in front of his house. It was true; the fresh air she had breathed in during the mostly silent ride from town had banished any lingering effects from the beer she'd sucked up earlier. "Why can't you just take me home?"

David shut off the engine and rested his forearms on the steering wheel. She sensed that he was studying her. Backlit by the front porch light and shaded by the brim of his baseball cap, his face was in shadow and his expression impossible to read.

The entire incident was just one more thing she would have to live down, but she wished David hadn't been the one to come after her.

"Let me fix you something to eat while you call home. They might be worried about you."

"I left a note on the kitchen counter," she replied.

"Did you want to wake them so they can read it?"

"Ha ha." His tone was dry.

She had always liked his voice, even when he was picking on her. Maturity had deepened it, roughed it up a little, so the sound of it stirred instead of soothed.

Ignoring its husky appeal, she folded her arms and stuck out her chin while she stared through the windshield. "I'm not hungry."

"Well, I am. You can keep me company."

"I'm not fit company," she argued, folding her arms. "I'm sloshed."

"You're exaggerating," he contradicted. "Besides, you don't eat enough." Gently he pinched her bare upper arm, making her yelp with surprise. "See?" he added. "No meat on your bones."

"What are you now, my mother?" she snapped to cover her flustered response to his brief touch.

"No, sweetie," he said softly. "I'm your friend."

His comment slapped her with guilt.

She wished she had the nerve to really shock him, to grab his face in her hands and plant a big wet kiss right on his mouth. Then she would stick out her chest and ask in a seductive whisper if he still wanted to be her pal. That ought to shut him up, to make him think twice about getting too close.

Of course, Kim didn't have the nerve or the confidence to pull off such a bold move. And maybe David didn't deserve to be treated like that anyway. After all, if he hadn't come down to the Longhorn, the bartender might have followed through on his threat to call her father.

Which didn't mean she was ready to weep tears

of gratitude all over the faded Dixie Chicks T-shirt that hugged David's wide chest. Instead she reached for the door handle of his killer red truck. The sight of it parked in front of the bar, all polished chrome, gleaming curves and wide tires, had been a reminder of just how little she knew about whatever fueled his dreams or made him tick.

"So what's on the menu tonight?" she asked, giving in to defeat.

"Come inside and find out."

From any other guy, she might have figured the comment for a lame pickup line, but with David she had no clue. While she fumbled with the door, he circled the truck. Just as he had when she climbed in at the Longhorn, he stuck out his hand to assist her.

"I'm okay." She stepped onto the narrow running board and then carefully down to the ground. A skirt and sandals with high, skinny heels would have made the maneuver a tricky one, but it was manageable in her stretchy black slacks and boots.

A big dog appeared from the shadows, startling her.

"Hey, Lulu." Looking unconcerned, David patted the animal's square head.

"Lulu?" Kim echoed, unable to stifle a smile.

At the sound of her name, the dog crowded closer and licked Kim's fingers.

"Lulu, behave." David grabbed her collar and glanced at Kim. "Sorry."

"It's okay." She offered her hand for the dog to sniff. Lulu's stub of a tail wagged so hard her hips shimmied.

"Where'd you get her?" Kim scratched behind

the floppy ears that didn't go with the shape of her head. "She's, um, unique."

"Robin found her at the shelter and decided I needed a watchdog. Your aunt can be very persuasive when she wants."

"I guess that doesn't surprise me," Kim replied. "She and I talked at dinner, and I got the impression that she's a very strong person."

"Just wait till you meet Calvin, my other roommate, also courtesy of our family veterinarian." David's tone was dry.

"So you've got two dogs?" She followed him up the steps, gripping the railing to combat a sudden wave of dizziness. Maybe he was right and she did need something to eat. Lunch had been an apple, and she had skipped dinner.

Taking a deep breath, she tried to ignore David's compact rear in well-worn denim as he climbed the steps ahead of her. It was obvious from the shape he was in that he spent most of his time doing hard physical labor.

"Calvin would be deeply offended by that question," David said over his shoulder as he opened the door and gestured for Kim to go into the house ahead of him. "He's a cat, but don't tell him that. He thinks he's a little person with fur who just happens to run this place."

"I like animals," she replied as she looked around.

"Calvin won't like me much if I don't remember to pick up his cat food at the clinic tomorrow. He's on a special diet."

A lamp had been left on low in the living room. David reached past her to switch on an overhead light. Lulu immediately walked over to a small rug beside the fireplace hearth and lay down with her homely head resting on her paws.

"Got any pets back in Seattle?" David asked.

"No. It's less complicated that way." She didn't add that Drew thought animals were dirty or that he loathed his mother's dogs. Secretly Kim had always suspected he was jealous.

No big-screen television or humongous entertainment center dominated David's living room, which looked comfortable and uncluttered. The furniture was nothing special: a couch in muted stripes, a couple of walnut end tables and a brown recliner that appeared to be real leather.

Through a wide arch was the dining room with a big window. A simple kitchen table and chairs were centered on a rag rug that complemented the hardwood floor. Above the table hung a brass light fixture.

She hovered, not sure what to do.

"You might as well come into the kitchen." David stopped abruptly and she nearly ran into him. "The bathroom's down that hall on the left, if you need it."

She glanced in the direction he pointed. "Is that the one that's all torn up?"

He looked surprised that she had remembered. "No, this one's intact." He glanced beneath the table. "Calvin must be asleep on my bed. You'll have to meet him next time."

If there is a next time, she thought.

The dining room walls were paneled with wood the color of honey. It matched the floor. A collection of branding irons hung next to some built-in shelves, empty except for a stack of paperbacks, two small trophies and a coffee mug. A pile of tack was heaped in one corner next to a pair of tooled leather boots. One had fallen over. The toes, she noticed, had silver tips.

Kim had forgotten what a pleasant little house this was. The original owner had built it himself, even the stone fireplace. Kim didn't know why he and her family hadn't gotten along, but she remembered how angry her father had been when he'd found out the old man had sold his place to Emily.

"What would you like? I've got canned soup, toast, or I could manage a grilled cheese sandwich without burning it."

"Not much of a cook?" she teased. The kitchen, like the other rooms she had seen, was clean and organized, but it certainly lacked a woman's influence.

She wasn't sure how the absence of those feminine touches made her feel. Sad, maybe, or indifferent, but certainly not relieved. Neither his house nor his life concerned her. She had left him behind in more ways than one, and there was no going back.

He leaned his hip against the tiled counter where a wood block held an impressive set of knives.

"Actually, I can cook a few things pretty well," he replied. "Otherwise I would have starved a long time ago." He rubbed his hands together, as though he were itching to impress her with his culinary talents. "So what will it be?"

"I told you I wasn't hungry," she reminded him. "Several times, in fact."

"Yeah, I heard you." A muscle flexed in his cheek and he looked down at his feet.

"So why did you insist on bringing me here, anyway?" She was getting tired. A headache tapped at her temples.

"I wondered why you went to the Longhorn," he said as he began making coffee. "It doesn't seem like your kind of place."

"Why not?" Kim glared at his back, resenting the way his wide shoulders tapered to a narrow waist above the tight butt she had done her best not to notice. Why couldn't he have grown up pudgy, with thinning hair and a nervous tick? "Perhaps I'm a lush," she added defiantly.

He didn't say anything until after he had the coffee going. "Not a chance." If he realized she hadn't answered his original question, he didn't comment.

She was itching to argue with someone, but her ineffective attorney wasn't here, nor was Drew's smug, superior mother, who had outmaneuvered Kim once again. The only one in range was David, calling himself her friend while he refused to give her a ride back to the main house.

"What makes you think you know so much about me?" she demanded, her frustration churning.

He gave her a level look that made her feel like a cranky child. "Joe Willy said you only had a few beers. A problem drinker holds her booze better than you."

"Oh." Suddenly Kim felt small for trying to antagonize him, and the last of her pleasant little buzz was dissipating like an early-morning fog. "I bet you have to get up with the roosters, so why don't we do this some other time?" Some time like never.

"Is this where I admit that I don't actually have any roosters, or should I just beat my chest and insist that I'm too tough to worry about a little missed sleep?'' he asked, arching his brow.

Not sure how to respond to his teasing, Kim opened the door to his refrigerator. She leaned in and scanned the contents.

''I can cook, too,'' she said. ''Since you're so determined to hold me hostage until I'm fed, why don't I fix us an omelet?'' Maybe then she could finally get out of here.

David studied the view she presented as she bent over, head in his fridge. Her shirt had hiked up, baring a thin line of skin between it and her snug black pants. A guy could get eye strain checking her out.

''You won't burn it?'' he asked absently.

''Cooking is one of my few accomplishments.'' Kim pulled open a crisper and hummed approvingly.

In short order an array of ingredients appeared on the counter; eggs, cheese, milk, butter, a chunk of ham, half a bell pepper and a couple of limp green onions. Intrigued, David got out the equipment she requested: bowl, whisk, paring knife, cutting board, grater, spatula, pan. For a few minutes they worked in relative harmony.

''I'm glad you're keeping it simple,'' he deadpanned as he stepped back and surveyed the cluttered counter. ''I was going to heat a can of soup.''

''What?'' Glancing up from the cheese she was grating, Kim blushed to the roots of her dark hair. ''Oh, gee, I'm so sorry!''

When he saw her distress, he became instantly contrite. ''I was kidding!''

He moved closer and cupped her shoulders. Beneath his hands he could feel the tension that hummed through her like a surge of electric current.

Did she never relax? No wonder she looked exhausted.

"Please, honey, don't be sorry about feeding us. Carry on with your magic. I'll make the toast and set the table."

Never mind that he hadn't been hungry. He would choke it down, even if her cooking made his own efforts taste like Wolfgang Puck's in comparison.

Kim either hadn't noticed the pet name that slipped out or she chose to ignore it as she went back to work. David kept quiet, afraid to upset her further. He couldn't help but wonder, though, what had happened to erode her self-esteem so badly.

Back in school she had been vibrant and cocky, despite the fact that she chafed constantly under Adam's strict parenting. David had been nuts about her, but he was afraid her interest in him had been just one more way of getting back at her father.

A few moments later, she dished up the omelet while he poured coffee and set a plate of toast on the table. After he'd held out her chair and they were both seated, he leaned toward his plate and took a tentative sniff. The appetizing aroma convinced him he was hungry after all.

"Smells good," he managed to say before he shoveled in the first forkful.

Ignoring her own food, Kim watched him chew and swallow.

"What's the matter?" he demanded, digging in. "Why aren't you eating?"

A tiny frown pinched the skin between her brows. "Is it really okay?"

David stared, his fork poised in midair. "Are you

kidding? It's great, believe me. Now eat up before it gets cold.''

"You're not just saying that?" she persisted.

He forced himself to set his fork back down. "Look, you told me you could cook, and you weren't lying. This is probably the best omelet I've ever had." He glanced around the dining room and ducked his head. "Sorry, Mom," he muttered, sneaking a glance at Kim, "but it's the truth."

Her chuckle sounded more like a hiccup, the kind someone makes when they don't know if they should laugh or cry. To his relief, she started eating.

Although he tried to slow down, it didn't take David long to finish. He only wished he could lick his plate, to get any specks he might have missed. Instead he munched on a slice of toast and watched Kim toy with her omelet. He nearly offered to help her finish it, but the point in dragging her over here hadn't been to fill *his* belly.

"That was fabulous," he exclaimed, pushing back his chair and toasting her with his coffee mug.

Kim had only taken a few bites when she laid down her fork. "Thank you," she mumbled, looking pleased.

"If I could, I'd hire you full-time," he added expansively.

Her smile widened, deepening the crease from the scar on her cheek.

"I don't work cheap." She touched a paper napkin to her mouth. "Too bad you can't afford me."

Several responses leaped to David's mind, none of them appropriate.

"Did your mother teach you to cook like this?" he asked curiously. Beyond the barest essentials, he knew nothing about Kim's life after she'd left the ranch.

One day she had been here, mad at Adam for something, as usual, and the next she was gone to live with her mother. David had waited, expecting an explanation. Finally he had broken down and made the first move, without success. By the time she finally came back to visit, he had become adept at avoidance and the next time he saw her, she was flashing Drew's ring.

His question about her cooking skills made her smile blink out as though a circuit had blown.

"Mom thought the microwave was the only appliance worth having, at least in the kitchen. After a while I got sick of that, so I started teaching myself."

She toyed with the handle of her coffee mug. "Drew gave me a gourmet cooking course for my birthday one year. Since we entertained a lot, he figured it would be a good investment. He even wrote it off as a business expense."

Picturing her as a married woman wasn't something David enjoyed doing. "That's nice."

Kim stacked their dirty dishes. "It's getting late, so I'll just wash these up and then you can run me home."

He leaned over and caught her wrist, preventing her from getting up. "Leave them, okay? I don't expect you to fix me a meal and then clean up, too."

Her eyes widened and her pulse jumped beneath his fingers. Reluctantly he let her go.

"You know how we do things around here," he reminded her. "If the women cook, the men do the KP."

"I guess I forgot." She scooted back her chair. "Let's both do it."

It only took a few minutes to load the dishes and utensils into the dishwasher, put the food away and wipe off the counter. Even though neither of them said anything, they worked together like a well-oiled machine, moving around each other without a single misstep. All the while, David tried to think of a way to get her to talk to him about what was troubling her. Something was wrong; the signs were getting more obvious.

Did your ex-husband abuse you? No, too direct. *Tell me again about that scar on your cheek.* Asked and answered. *Want to see my bedroom?*

Whoa! Now he was getting sidetracked. Derailed. A total fatality.

Kim was watching him with a puzzled frown as she wiped her hands on the kitchen towel hanging from the handle of the oven door. "What's wrong?"

He had wanted to ask her the same question. Perhaps he was jumping to a lot of conclusions, reading things that weren't there into the behavior of a woman he'd barely spoken to for ten years. All he could really do at this point was to try to gain her trust, in case she had no one else to talk to, and to get the physical pull he felt toward her back under control before she picked up on it and shut him out completely.

"I was just wondering why the omelet you fixed tonight was so much better than mine ever are," he replied with an easy grin.

To his relief, she smiled back at him. "That's my secret." She tossed her head as she strutted toward the front door, hips shifting sweetly.

When he caught up to her, he handed her a folded piece of paper. "My phone number and my cell, in case you need to get hold of me." When she reached for the paper, he held on to it for a second before letting it go. "Don't hesitate, okay? I mean it."

"Thanks." She tucked the numbers into her purse, but she didn't offer hers in return.

Trust takes time, he reminded himself, and he had all the time in the world.

"You surprise me," she said when they were both seated in the truck and he'd fired up the engine.

"Why?" Had he failed to hide his reaction to her as well as he had hoped? Would she be amused, or just dismayed that he hadn't learned his lesson a long time ago? Braced for either her scorn or her pity, he switched on the headlights and looked at her warily in the glow from the dash as he shifted into Reverse.

She gestured at the expanse of controls and gauges and the killer stereo system he'd had installed. "I never pictured you as a monster truck kind of guy."

Surprised that she even had an opinion about what he might drive, he still didn't think he wanted to know what it was—sensible sedan? Rusted-out beater? Or maybe just an old work truck with a two-tone paint job, a mismatched fender, a few redneck bumper stickers and lots of dents.

When he didn't respond, she continued anyway. "Being an ex-L.A. type, I figured you'd be driving a hot sports car, a convertible with fancy wheels and a leather interior." She smoothed her hand along the edge of her seat. "Well, I got one thing right."

He barely resisted the urge to puff out his chest and preen. "A couple of the old-timers still call me L.A.," he said instead.

"You weren't born in Elbert County," she replied. "To some folks, you could own this ranch, but you'd still be an outsider."

David looked at her and swallowed hard. He had to remind himself that she'd been married to a successful attorney. It wasn't faded jeans and scuffed boots she found attractive, it was money and power. David hadn't kept her from leaving, and he wasn't the reason she had come back.

"Well, it's pretty difficult to haul a horse trailer behind a 'Vette," he drawled as he went through the front gate to the ranch. "A truck's more practical."

She ran her hand over the console. "Sweetheart, there ain't nothin' practical about this rig."

He gripped the wheel hard, struggling to ignore the way her words and her husky tone affected him, when all he wanted to do was to turn the truck around and take her back to his place. Damn, but he needed to get out more.

On countless other mornings, he had come over before first light, driving down the other branch to the rutted road. Ranchers got up early and went to bed early. With any luck, they would all sleep right through the familiar sound from his engine, even if their dogs didn't.

He slowed to a crawl and sneaked past Travis's house. In the yellow glow from a yard light, the Irish setter on the porch lifted its head to watch them, but he didn't bother to raise an alarm.

"What are you going to tell the folks about their car if they notice that it's missing before I get it back?" he asked. "You know word will get to Adam that it sat in town overnight."

She was looking out the side window. "I hadn't really thought about it."

"Have you got a car back in Seattle?" he asked idly.

She nodded silently.

"What are you going to do with it if you stay here? Sell it?"

"Drew bought it, so Drew got to keep it." The brittle tone was back in her voice. "Not that he actually wanted it, of course, since a Sterling wouldn't be caught dead behind the wheel of a *used* car unless it was some kind of rare restored classic." Tossing her head, she ran her hand through her short hair. "He'd rather put my car in a crusher than let me keep it, so he's welcome to it." She tipped her head from side to side, stretching the kinks from her neck. "Maybe he'll donate it somewhere. His family's big on charitable contributions, as long as they're tax deductible."

David didn't know what to say as he pulled into the driveway, and he still didn't know if she was staying.

"It doesn't sound as though the two of you parted friends," he ventured, fishing shamelessly.

"It's hard to stay friends with someone who blames you for losing his heir." She pushed open her door before David could react.

"You had a miscarriage?" he asked.

She nodded, lips pressed together as though she already regretted telling him.

"I'm sorry." The news shocked and saddened him as he tried to picture her big with someone else's child and failed.

"It doesn't matter." Her voice had changed from hot to chilly. "Thanks for the ride."

Why, oh, why had she told David about losing her baby, she berated herself silently as she sneaked into the house, trying to make as little noise as possible. She eased the heavy door shut behind her and leaned against it, scarcely breathing as she listened to the throaty rumble of the retreating engine.

She hadn't wanted anyone here to know, so why hadn't she kept her lips zipped? If he let anything slip to the family, they'd be hurt that she hadn't been the one to tell them.

Had she wanted to shock him, to justify herself, or just to tell someone who might not blame her? Ever since that last hurtful argument with Drew and his terrible accusations, she had kept her feelings tucked away. Now her disappointment and sadness were fresh again, smarting like a sore with the scab ripped off.

As she slipped off her boots, she wondered what David thought of her after tonight, a boozer who couldn't stay pregnant.

The porch light shone through the beveled-glass windows flanking the double front doors, keeping the entry from being totally dark. Old habits prompted Kim to peek into the living room to see if her father waited in the shadows for her to come home, as he had when she was young.

At first she thought she was hallucinating when she saw him sitting on the couch. She blinked hard a couple of times and looked again, genuinely surprised that he was still there.

"Hi, Kimmie," he said quietly as he got to his feet. "Is everything okay?"

"I'm fine, thank you. What are you doing here in the dark? Is your leg bothering you?" Maybe, just maybe he hadn't been waiting for her after all.

"I got your note," he said. "It's been a long time since I used to wait up for you. Do you remember?"

"Of course I do." She cleared her throat. "I'm sorry I took the car without saying anything first, and I hope that didn't cause you or Emily any inconvenience."

He made a dismissive gesture with his hand. "There are a lot of wheels around here if we need a set, so don't worry about it. Why did David bring you home?"

She managed a chuckle that came out a little strained. "It's complicated and I'm really tired, okay? He said he'd get your car in the morning."

She wished her father would move closer so she could see his face more clearly. Perhaps then she could get some idea what he was thinking.

"Why don't you come in and sit down for a few minutes," he suggested. "We could talk, like old times."

They had never talked, or at least he hadn't listened to her, not really. He'd been too busy tossing out rules. Now that he'd finally found the time to listen, the tables had turned and she was no longer interested.

She moved toward the staircase. "I'm sorry," she said quietly, careful to keep any hint of animosity from her tone, "it's really too late."

If he misinterpreted her words, that was his problem. It had stopped mattering to her a long time ago.

"All right," he said softly. "Good night, then."

She echoed his sentiment and went up the stairs in the dark. She knew the way by heart, even knew what the fifteen darker squares that lined the wall were—photographs of her, one for each year she had lived here with him.

When she reached the top of the stairs, she stifled a yawn. The entire evening had been an emotional roller-coaster ride, and she was worn-out. Jake and Cheyenne were both sleeping soundly behind their closed bedroom doors. Kim hoped she would be able to do the same, because tomorrow she needed the energy to figure out what to do with the rest of her life.

Chapter Six

Dawn was an expanding glow on the eastern horizon when David walked into the bunkhouse later that morning, stifling a yawn behind his hand. The other men had already eaten the huge breakfast Cookie prepared every morning except Sundays, and the long tables were cleared off.

Adam handed out the work assignments for the day while the men finished their coffee. Several of them nodded to David when he sat down, but Adam's only acknowledgment was to glance up from his clipboard with raised brows. Travis, the cow boss, was standing next to him. He gave David a wink.

On most mornings David ate here, too, but today he had overslept. After he'd taken Kim home, he had lain awake for a long time, thinking about the bombshell she had dropped before she got out of his truck and hurried into the house.

She'd had a miscarriage and her husband blamed her for it. The guy was beginning to sound like a real bastard.

The girl David knew would never be capable of doing anything to put her pregnancy at risk. There was no possibility that she had changed that much, not in ten years or ten lifetimes.

"Mr. Major! You with us, or are you still sleeping?" Adam's voice sliced across David's thoughts, the mocking formality a sure sign that the boss was ticked.

When David saw the men's smirks, his face got hot and he knew he'd be in for a ribbing later. At least no one had said anything about him dropping Kim off earlier.

"Sorry, boss," he said apologetically. "I'm awake now."

There were a couple more chuckles and one noisy yawn that was quickly stifled when Adam's annoyed expression didn't change.

"I asked if you felt up to taking your crew out to move those steers in from the northeast pasture." His tone oozed exaggerated patience, but David was well aware he had little tolerance for tardiness.

Perhaps it was more than that. David swallowed hard, wondering if Adam had heard Kim come in. Did he still think David wasn't good enough for her?

He would need to borrow one of the guys to go into town with him and pick up the car, but he wasn't about to announce that in front of everyone.

"Uh, could I talk to you about that, boss?" he asked instead.

For a moment Adam just looked at him. Then Travis turned his back to the room and said something meant only for his older brother's ears. Adam's attention stayed on David, who tried not to squirm.

"Okay, see me when we're done here," Adam told him gruffly.

David might be a foreman and a stepson, but neither position ever cut him any slack with the brothers when it came to running the W. Normally that was the way he preferred it. He'd earned his spot and he deserved it, working after school and every summer vacation, then coming back full-time after getting his degree.

Stomach rumbling, he helped himself to a fat, fragrant cinnamon roll and a mug of the black sludge that Cookie referred to as coffee, while he waited for the rest of the work to be assigned and questions answered.

"Engine trouble?" Cookie asked as he put away the ham he'd sliced off for sandwiches. His helper was busy washing the mountain of dirty dishes and pans.

"Overslept," David mumbled, mouth full of pastry. He must have finally drifted off about the time he usually got up. If Lulu hadn't barked in his ear, he'd still be in the sack.

Maybe Sam and Buck could ride out with a couple of the cattle dogs and start moving the stock while Tony went to town with David. They'd be back in time to catch up with the others.

Travis and his men grabbed their sack lunches and left to collect the rest of their gear. A couple of them glanced back with open curiosity on their grizzled faces as Adam motioned David away from the tables.

"Have you seen Kim?" David asked, before Adam could say anything. "How's she doing?"

The older man's eyes narrowed and he folded his arms across his chest. "Why don't you tell me?"

David had hoped to find out how much Adam knew. It was no surprise the older man usually came out a winner at their monthly poker games, because he never let anything show that he didn't intend to.

"Sounds like she's had a difficult time lately," David said carefully, trying to get a peek at Adam's cards while keeping his own hand hidden. "It's good that she came home."

A muscle jumped in Adam's cheek, but he remained silent, while David could feel sweat beading on his forehead despite the cool morning air. He'd seen Adam use the same level stare on countless occasions, a ploy that usually resulted in the recipient spilling every sin he'd ever committed. David gritted his teeth and tried not to appear guilty—of anything.

"Where's my car?" Adam asked, hooking his thumbs into his wide leather belt.

"Didn't you see Kim's note? She told me she left it on the kitchen counter."

"I saw it, and then I saw her when she got home." As usual, the older man's expression was unreadable. "Does looking out for her have anything to do with being her stepbrother?"

"No, sir," David replied. Kim was an adult now, and so was he. Adam had kept her from dating as a teenager, but the only one who was going to tell David to leave her alone this time around was Kim.

"That's what I thought," Adam said. "Take Tony with you to get your mom's car back, and don't be all day." He turned away, but then he glanced back over his shoulder as David let out the breath he'd been holding.

"She's fragile," he added quietly. "I can't think of anyone I'd rather have watching out for her than you."

Too stunned by the comment to move, David watched his mentor walk out the door. His vision blurred. Blinking hard, he glanced sheepishly around to see if anyone had noticed, but Cookie and his helper were hard at work in the kitchen. Relieved, David went to catch Tony before he saddled up.

After she had showered and dressed in an oversize T-shirt and cutoff jeans, Kim stood in her bedroom doorway and strained her ears for sounds from the rest of the house. When all she heard was silence, she crept down the stairs in search of some coffee and maybe a piece of fruit.

She'd heard the younger kids talking about going to play at Aunt Rory's, so Emily was probably already working in her studio behind the main house. Kim hoped that David had made good on his promise to bring home the car.

The kitchen had been cleaned up from breakfast and it was empty except for the coffeepot. Breathing a silent prayer of gratitude for the caffeine and the solitude, she unhooked a mug from the metal tree sitting on the granite counter. She didn't really feel like dealing with anyone yet.

"Oh, there you are." Emily appeared suddenly in the doorway from the wing where the laundry room and the ranch office were located. "How are you?"

Startled, Kim spilled a few drops of the coffee she'd been pouring. "I'm fine, thanks." She figured Emily had heard about last night's escapade by now and must be curious about her son's part in it.

"Want a refill?" Kim held up the pot to distract her.

"No, thanks. I'm cutting back." Emily got down a glass and poured water from the dispenser instead.

Kim decided to forget about getting something to eat. She could drink her coffee in her room while she decided how to spend her day.

"Can I fix you something?" Emily offered. "There's pancake batter left, if you don't mind chocolate chips." She wrinkled her nose. "That's what Chey and Jake wanted, even though it sounds more like dessert than breakfast to me." She was wearing pink shorts and a matching plaid shirt, with her hair pulled into a clip on top of her head.

"No, thanks," Kim replied, sipping her coffee. "I don't think the words chocolate and pancakes really belong in the same sentence."

Emily laughed, clearly delighted. "Oh, honey, I have to agree, and you're talking to a woman who's never found a chocolate calorie she didn't like, and vice versa."

She pulled out a bar stool and sat down as if she had all the time in the world. "Do you have everything you need?"

The question made Kim feel like a guest, and then she realized that was exactly what she was.

"Yes, thanks for getting my bedroom ready for me." She hesitated, not wanting to appear rude by leaving the room. "Aren't you working on something?" she finally blurted out.

Emily had a widespread reputation as a rare-book restorer. As well as several museums, an impressive list of wealthy clients entrusted her with their family treasures and priceless collections. Even Kim was impressed by the meticulous restoration she performed on crumbling tomes, matching the print fonts and even the glue formulas exactly.

Now she waved her fingers in a gesture of dismissal. "I'm waiting for several of my current projects to dry," she said. "And I'm expecting a shipment of marbled paper that's way overdue."

Kim didn't know what to say, so she merely smiled and nodded.

"Got time to help me bake a few pies this morning?" Emily asked unexpectedly. "Mrs. Crow from down the road brought over some really nice peaches earlier. I'd like to get them in the oven before it's time to fix lunch."

Kim was about to refuse, but then something stopped her. What else did she have to do today except to think about the mess she'd made of her life, and kick herself for telling David about the miscarriage? The last thing she wanted from him was pity. Besides, she should have offered to make herself useful before now.

"Sure. Maybe you can show me how to make a decent pie crust. Mine either falls apart or comes out tough."

For the next little while, the two women, both wearing colorful aprons supplied by Emily, discussed baking and other generalities while Kim peeled and sliced the peaches and Emily assembled everything else they needed. A couple of times Kim even found herself laughing at the cooking disaster stories her stepmother told of herself. Kim knew from what David had told her before that Emily's first husband, his father, was extremely successful. They'd lived in a huge house in southern California, complete with its own staff.

"I enjoyed cooking whenever I was allowed in my kitchen, so I knew the basics before I moved here," Emily said as she set out flour, sugar and oil. "Luckily, you can feed a growing boy spaghetti, casseroles and lasagna without him complaining too much, because his biggest concern is quantity, but providing for a hardworking husband and an expanded family is something else again."

"How did you learn?" Kim asked, cutting into another peach and removing the pit. "Did you take a class?"

"From who?" Emily replied. "Colorado women seem born knowing how to cook."

"Not this one," Kim drawled. "My ex bought me a gourmet cooking course."

"I guess that even jerks have to eat."

Her comment startled Kim, who didn't know what to say.

"I learned by trial and error," Emily said "Plus TV cooking shows, a few bad recipes, some burned meals and lots of antacid tablets. Your dad made a great guinea pig, but I'll deny it if you tell him I said that." She got out a big mixing bowl. "How did you like the cooking class?"

Kim described some of the dishes they'd fixed. To her relief, Emily didn't use her comments as a launching pad for personal questions.

"Let's get the crust ready," she said. "The secret of a good pie crust is cold water and as little overstirring, overrolling and overfussing as possible."

Eventually they had two pies assembled and safely baking in the wall oven. Some of Emily's hair had escaped its scrunchy to fall in attractive wisps around her face, and she had a smudge of flour on her chin. Kim hadn't fared any better, her hands sticky and peach juice smeared on the front of her blouse above her apron.

"Your father will be just as appreciative of your help as am I." Emily wiped flour and bits of crust off the marble insert in the counter while the sink filled with water. "You're well aware that peach is his favorite."

Usually Kim viewed that kind of comment as Emily's attempt to show that she knew Kim's father better than Kim did, but this time she realized it was probably the other woman's way of trying to find common ground. Up until now, Kim's father was the only apparent interest that she and her stepmother shared, but that was probably Kim's fault. She'd never made much effort, even after she got over her initial resentment of Emily.

Every time Kim remembered her childish attitude when she walked into the stable and caught her father kissing Emily, she wanted to sink through the floor with embarrassment. No wonder he had stood up for Emily, treating Kim like the brat she'd been and sending her to her room.

She was only now beginning to realize that the rift she'd created that night with her father had never really healed; it had only grown over. Shortly after that incident, she had gone to live in Denver with her mother.

"The housekeeper, Betty Clark, used to bake peach cobbler for Daddy when I was little," Kim volunteered as she wiped her hands. "She always let me help."

"So you're an old hand at peeling peaches?" Emily finished running water into the other sink and began washing the utensils they'd used.

Kim had to chuckle. "No way was Mrs. Clark going to let me near a paring knife and risk Daddy's wrath. I made cinnamon-butter doodles with the leftover crust."

"He was protective of you and she was probably scared of him," Emily said. "His temper can be, um, formidable."

"I think you've got that wrong," Kim replied. "Daddy was a lot more scared of Mrs. Clark than she ever was of him." The memory of the housekeeper shaking her finger under his nose while she scolded him, all the while refusing to comply with his repeated requests that she call him by his first name because it would be too familiar, made Kim smile.

"She passed away last year." She blinked away sudden tears. "I was sorry to miss the funeral." Drew had forbidden her to miss his parents' anniversary party. Although she had complied to avoid an ugly scene, she'd resented his attitude.

"There was quite a turnout at the church," Emily said gently. "It sounds like you have some nice memories of her, though, and that's what's really important."

The front door burst open, followed by the sounds of a scuffle.

"I beat you!" Jake's voice preceded him down the hallway, followed by Cheyenne's wail of protest.

"You pushed me out of the way!" Her voice rose. "That's cheating and I'm telling Mom."

Kim looked at Emily with mingled regret over the

interruption and surprise that she had enjoyed their visit so much. "It's been fun."

Emily smoothed her hands down her apron while Kim removed hers and handed it back. "For me, too, but now playtime is over." Her grin widened as she shook a mocking finger. "I'll tell your dad that you helped with the pies, but I'm not admitting that I let you use a knife."

David headed toward the highway in his pickup, almost pitifully grateful the long day was over. After he got back from town, he'd spent most of it in the saddle, so he was tired, dirty and smelled of horse. While he'd been musing over whether Kim gave last night a passing thought, he'd mashed his thumb between a fence post and a stubborn heifer. His thumb still throbbed dully, keeping the beat with Dwight Yoakam jamming hard on the cranked-up stereo he viewed as a necessary upgrade.

David longed for a hot shower and a cold beer, not necessarily in that order, before he fed himself and his animals, finished setting the tile trim around the tub and fell into bed.

He hoped there was a pizza in the freezer for his dinner and a clean work shirt for morning. His mother would willingly do his laundry if he asked, would fill his freezer with food if he let her and would happily set him up with the daughters of her friends if she thought the payoff might be grandchildren to spoil. So far he'd resisted all three, but after days like this he was beginning to weaken on the laundry issue.

A frisky yearling in the pasture by the road kicked up its heels and raced his truck down the fence line.

Grinning, David backed off on the pedal to give the bay colt an edge. It beat him by a nose, then bucked a few times, the equine version of chest beating for his buddies.

David was still grinning and singing with Dwight when he noticed Kim walking back down the road from the mailbox. All his aches and scrapes disappeared, sore thumb forgotten, and his mood hitched up a notch or six. She was wearing her usual tan pants, one of her loose white shirts that failed to completely hide the sway of her narrow hips, and a straw hat with a wide brim. Not as blatantly sexy as the outfit she'd worn to the Longhorn, but good enough. Mindful of the dust, he slowed down even more, his windows open to the breeze.

As he crawled up alongside her, she lifted her hand holding the mail in a laconic greeting and stepped off the road so he could go on by. He stopped instead, turning down the music and leaning out the window.

"Hey, beautiful," he said. "You don't look hung over to me. How are you feeling?"

She shrugged. "Good enough. Thanks for bringing back the car."

"No problem. Climb in and I'll run you to the house."

She looked up and down the road, then shrugged again. "Okay, but you've got to switch that music, country boy."

Wiping his brow on his forearm, he leaned over to open her door. "What's your pleasure, Seattle grunge?"

Her lips twitched. "Do you live in a time warp,

cowboy? That is so over with, it's not even worth discussing.''

"So what did you tell Adam?" he asked after she'd settled next to him. He turned at the Y and headed toward the rise, hoping he didn't reek too badly.

Her creamy skin was free of last night's makeup, her lashes dark as coal dust and her naked lips sexy as hell.

David's reaction was sudden, unwelcome and distinctly uncomfortable.

"Tell him about what?" She settled against the passenger door, facing him, and arched one delicate brow.

Hearing the warning in her tone, David figured a change of subject might be prudent. "Never mind. Did you sleep all day?"

Her mouth relaxed into a smile and he nearly drove off the road before he straightened the wheel.

"I spent the morning baking pies with your mom. If you ask her nicely, she'd maybe give you a sample."

If he asked Kim nicely, would *she* give him a sample? Not in this lifetime, he'd bet.

"You and my mom spent time together?" he blurted out, sounding less than tactful. Everyone liked his mother, but Kim had stopped at polite a long time ago.

Now she reached up to stroke the miniature dream catcher that hung from the mirror, a gift from a girl whose name he'd forgotten. The faded ribbon was an indication of how much time had passed since the two of them had parted company for reasons as vague as her face.

"I sliced the peaches a neighbor brought by," Kim said lightly. "It was actually kind of fun. Then Chey and Jake came in, so we all had lunch together."

"They're good kids." He was still driving as slow as a turtle stampede, making the time last and wondering whether she had noticed. "I'm taking the two of them to the fair on Saturday. Want to come along and help ride herd?"

She pursed her lips, making his breath catch. He had kissed those lips a few times, touched her breast once, accidentally on purpose, and made her the star of some adolescent dreams. Now he figured she was going to refuse his invitation, but she gave the dream catcher a spin.

"Throw in some cotton candy and I'm yours for the day."

Was she flirting with him? The notion made his mind seize like an old engine.

"As much as you want," he said fervently. "I'll even throw in a corn dog."

"Well, okay then. I'm yours."

He could have leaned across the seat to nibble his way up her stem of a neck to her ears and then suck the lobes for a couple of days, but he knew he stunk of work. They were also parked in his boss's driveway, not the best setting for seduction.

He settled for promising to let her know what time they'd be leaving, then reversing slowly when she went inside. He maintained a death grip on the steering wheel and a stately pace until he hit the main highway. Then he floored the engine and slapped the wheel hard. Even the immediate jab of discomfort from his tender thumb wasn't enough to dampen his mood.

"I want to see the bunnies first," Cheyenne exclaimed from the back seat of Emily's sedan. "And I'd like a hot dog and a funnel cake, please."

"No way! Dumb rabbits are for babies!" Jake cried. "First *I* want to go—"

"They're not, either! And I'm not a baby!" Cheyenne's voice had a dangerous wobble, signaling imminent tears.

Kim was already beginning to regret agreeing to spend the entire day with them, and with David. She was getting too involved. Something of her second thoughts must have shown on her face, because he reached over and patted her hand as he glanced into the rearview mirror.

"Kids, what did I tell you about arguing?" he asked calmly.

The back seat of his mother's car went silent. Where had he learned how to pull off that trick?

"I'm still waiting." As he drove toward the county seat and the fairgrounds in Kiowa, he kept glancing in the mirror. "Shall I pull off the road while we discuss getting along?"

"No!" they cried in unison as Kim turned to look at them.

"You promised we'd have time to do everything we want, so there's no reason for us to argue," Cheyenne recited with an angelic expression as she skewered her brother with a sideways look.

Kim had no practical experience growing up with siblings. When she thought of Chey and Jake, her mind lumped them with Travis's children and Charlie's new baby, as kin, nieces and nephews, as part of a sea of faces in an expanding family. It was hard to remember that the two riding in the back seat were of course much more directly related to her than the others.

She would have liked to ask them what kind of a parent was the father they shared—strict, intimidating, rigid, patient, generous?—but she knew the question would only confuse them. They had no reference point, no comparison except their boisterous uncles and the parents of their friends.

"Well, I'm not sure about seeing *everything,*" David finally replied with a dry chuckle, "but we'll certainly do our best, depending on how well your sister's feet hold up."

That rat, dumping it all on Kim!

"What's wrong with Chey's feet?" Jake demanded.

"No, silly," she hissed in a stage whisper, "he's talking about Kim. She's your sister, too."

"Oh, yeah, I forgot," Jake muttered.

It sounded to Kim as if the notion of being half siblings was as hard for them to grasp as it was for her. Not that she had made much effort to be a part of their lives beyond dutiful cards and presents on the appropriate occasions. Last Christmas she and Drew had sent Cheyenne a velvet dress and patent leather shoes! How far off the mark had that choice been?

Kim sat back and bent her knee so she could stick her foot up high enough for it to be seen from the back seat. It earned her a startled glance from the driver.

"See?" she demanded, wiggling her foot as the two kids giggled loudly. "I wore comfy shoes, so my feet will be just fine." She eyed David's western boots. "We'll just see who gives out first."

"Is that a challenge?" he asked softly.

"You betcha." She had decided when she got up this morning to enjoy the break from the decisions and concerns that shadowed her. For the second time this week she had even ignored her self-imposed rule to keep her appearance low-key. She was sure to run into former classmates and acquaintances who might have heard she was back, and was still vain enough to care what impression she made.

"You look real nice," David said as though he had been reading her mind. "I like that color on you. It matches your eyes."

"Why, thank you." Kim glanced down at the light-green cropped shirt and striped shorts she was wearing. "Even though your shirt doesn't match *your* eyes, you look real nice, too."

"His shirt is orange!" Jake exclaimed. "No one has eyes that color."

David was wearing a Broncos T-shirt, blue jeans and a ball cap with the team logo, a birthday present Jake had been quick to take credit for. The casual uniform of the Colorado male at play was a far cry from the eclectic wardrobe David had brought with him from L.A. when he first arrived to wow the hayseeds; vintage bowling shirts, baggy pants, Hawaiian prints and pricey athletic shoes that most of the local kids had only seen in magazines. It hadn't taken long for him to realize he might make friends more quickly if he didn't stand out from the high school crowd like a slightly bizarre peacock.

No longer would David have to bother wearing odd clothes to attract attention, Kim acknowledged silently as she studied his profile. Maturity and hard work had deepened his chest and broadened his shoulders. His height and his face were bound to attract feminine stares from one end of the county to the other.

She hadn't heard any mention of a girlfriend, which made her curious. Didn't he want a family of his own someday? A little dynasty to rival that of his stepfamily?

"Look! I can see the Ferris wheel!" Jake shouted from the back seat. He was bouncing with excitement.

"Does it bring back memories?" David asked Kim.

The two of them had gone to a rodeo with a group from school, but she'd missed the fair that year. Had he taken someone else?

"Sure it does," she replied as they joined the line of pickups and cars crawling toward the fairground entrance. "I came here a lot when I was a kid."

"I bet they don't have any cool fairs in Seattle." Cheyenne's tone dripped scorn.

Kim turned around. "Actually, they have a huge fair in Puyallup every year, with a lot of the same cool stuff they have here, and several others, too. We're not as uncivilized as you seem to think."

"*Pew*-allup," Jake mimicked, making his sister laugh.

"You still say 'we,'" David commented. "Does that mean you're planning to go back eventually?"

His question put Kim on the spot. "I haven't decided."

"Can we come and visit you there?" Chey asked.

"You and Jake came to Seattle for my wedding," Kim replied. "You were too little to remember."

David's smile faded as he stared straight ahead. Was he sorry that it hadn't worked out for her, or was he recalling the appendectomy that had kept him from making the trip?

"I've seen your picture," Cheyenne said importantly. "You had a pretty dress and a long veil, just like a bride on top of a wedding cake."

"Thank you, sweetie." Kim sneaked a glance at David. "That was the look I was aiming for."

He seemed preoccupied as he drove into the parking area, a muscled jumping along his jaw as though his teeth were clenched. It had to be the appendectomy.

"The groom was so handsome in the pictures. He had blond hair, like a movie star, and he was wearing a black suit," Chey added.

"That's called a tuxedo," Kim corrected her, hoping for distraction. The last thing she wanted was to relive the details of the huge, professionally orchestrated wedding that Drew and his mother had insisted was the only proper way for him and his bride to embark on their matrimonial voyage.

What a poor investment it had turned out to be for all concerned.

After David parked the car and bought the tickets, he and Kim walked inside with the children between them, holding hands in a string. All around them people hurried along like lemmings heading for the cliffs and the sea far below. Jake skipped with each step. Cheyenne chattered nonstop about last year's fair with David and some girl named Denise, but at least she'd dropped the subject of Kim's wedding.

They must look like a real family to anyone who didn't know them, Kim thought.

Once they got inside, David called a halt, program in hand. "Okay," he said. "What's first?"

"I have to go to the bathroom," Chey announced loudly, as a white-haired woman walking by caught Kim's eye.

"Some things never change," the woman said with a friendly smile. "Kids and bathrooms."

They had trouped through the exhibits of home-made pickles and homegrown produce, canned fruit and beef jerky, cookies, candy and holiday bread. They had viewed shiny tractors, pole buildings and knitting machines, watched a demo of slicing and dicing, heard a spiel about lifetime siding. They'd breathed in the smoke from the barbecue pit, smelled the animals and the food. They'd eaten way too much. They saw pigs, goats, rabbits, chickens, horses, sheep and breeds of cattle David didn't know existed.

He was more than ready to turn the kids loose on the carnival rides with a fistful of tickets while he and Kim put their feet up, sipped cold lemonade and kept a watchful eye.

It only took a few minutes to accomplish all three.

He escorted her to a picnic table in the shade of the grandstand with a clear view of the carnival. A band was playing nearby, and the air was perfumed with the scent of fresh caramel corn.

"Are you sure you don't want to go on that bungie drop?" David asked innocently.

Kim looked at the towering structure, her neck a

graceful stem that held up her close-cropped head. "I'm right behind you."

Way up at the top, two men were strapping a volunteer into the chair that David assumed would then plummet into the netting stretched below. He couldn't fathom why anyone wanted to pay to be terrified. Briefly he debated whether calling her bluff was worth risking his life.

"After everything I put in my stomach, I don't think I want to risk it." He waved his permission to the kids, who'd just gotten off the Tilt-a-whirl and were pointing at the haunted house while a vampire beckoned from the rickety steps.

Kim lowered her head and made a noise that sounded suspiciously like a chicken clucking. "I know you're just making excuses, but you're really as yellow as the roast corn they're selling down the row."

"May I remind you that in addition to the roast corn, I've had a hot dog, an elephant ear, a cookie the size of a hubcap and part of a caramel apple that Chey couldn't finish," David said indignantly. Just reciting the list made him queasy. He pressed a hand to his gut.

"Wimp!" Her eyes sparkled with laughter, catching his breath in his throat. "Jake ate more than you."

A thin high scream drew their attention to the brave soul who'd been dropped about half a mile from the top of the tower into the safety net below. A cluster of waiting teenage boys hooted, clapped and whistled shrilly while he flopped like a trout trying to right himself.

The poor kid would pay for that scream for a week, David thought with a twinge of compassion.

"You didn't eat much. Why don't you go first?" he asked Kim. Damn, but he hoped she was scared of heights. If she accepted, the kid being helped out of the net wasn't the only one in for a ribbing. David would be right there in the fools' gallery next to him.

"It was your idea, tough guy." Kim tossed her head. "I wouldn't dream of cutting in line."

"Did I mention the super-size burger and the double order of curly fries I had when you and Chey were looking at quilts and all that other girly stuff?" he asked hopefully.

Her eyes narrowed as she sipped her lemonade, lips puckered. "You led us to believe that you and Jake had been trying to win your mom a stuffed animal at the ring toss!"

David looked away. "I guess I forgot about the burger."

"Uh-huh. Will he back up your story?" she asked suspiciously.

He could hardly choke down his laughter. "Honey, after today, I own Jake. He'll say anything I want. Where he's concerned, I'm golden."

Kim shook her head. "What you are is shameless."

It was nice to see her having such a good time, even though all she'd had to eat was one scone, a bottle of water and an ice cream cone. Watching her licking it up had nearly been his undoing. He'd had to walk away for a minute and suck in a few deep breaths.

The day wasn't over yet. There was still the rodeo later on, if Jake and Chey held up that long.

The kids in question came running up to the picnic table, both wearing huge smiles on their sticky faces.

"Can we go on the roller coaster?" Jake asked.

The structure was easy to see from their table. It wasn't big, just a portable ride that was part of the traveling carnival.

Fondly, he looked at Cheyenne. Her hair was a mess and her mouth was ringed with ice cream. There were smudges on her shirt and a streak of dirt on her cheek, but she was dancing with excitement.

"You sure you want to ride the coaster?" he asked her.

She jumped up and down, clapping her hands together. "Yes, please!"

David drew out the moment by looking at Kim. "We-ell," he teased. "What do you think?"

Playing along, she pressed her lips together and narrowed her eyes till they were only a wink of green. "Looks pretty scary."

"Not to us," Jake insisted.

"It's really just little," Cheyenne added. "No big kids are even riding it, honest, 'cuz it's not scary enough."

"In that case, maybe you should go with them." Kim gave David an innocent smile. "Since it's so little and all."

He tried to look offended, but failed totally to keep himself from returning her grin. "Next year," he promised. "I'll have to work up to it."

She hooted. "Uh-huh."

"Got enough tickets?" he asked the kids.

They counted what was left.

"Okay, that'll be the last ride for today." He'd spent a small fortune, but their grins were worth every penny. "Come straight back here the minute you're done."

"Can we look at the arcade games on our way?" Jake asked. "We'll stay together, I promise."

David made them both cross their hearts. Maybe it was just a small county fair, but times were changing. Strangers were moving into the new housing developments that were starting to spring up. "Don't be too long."

"You're so good with them," Kim said after they'd left again. "Do you stay in touch with your other half brother, too?"

David traced an imaginary circle on the table with his finger, struggling against the familiar wash of guilt.

"Since my father and Stephanie split up and I'm not in contact with him anymore, I've kind of lost touch with Zane, too," he admitted.

"How old is he now?" She appeared genuinely curious. What a complicated blended family they had between them.

"Stephanie had Zane right before Mom and I moved out here, so he must be ten now," David calculated. "I feel sorry for the little guy. Dad's been a real bust as a father to me, and I'm sure he's no better with Zane."

He didn't have to explain it to Kim. She'd known how desperately David had counted on going back to Brentwood that first summer to see his friends, how crushed he'd been when his father had used the excuse of a heavy work schedule to casually beg off. Thank God that Adam had stepped in to offer him a part-time job at the ranch, despite his misgivings about David coming within ten miles of his only off-spring at the time, Kim.

Knowing how indifferent Stuart Major could be, how preoccupied with business and golf and everything else except his family, David felt he should have made a bigger effort with Zane all along.

"I never thought much about how humiliated your mother must have been, and how heartbroken over being replaced by a younger woman. Especially when she found out Stephanie was already pregnant when Stuart asked for the divorce." Kim finished her lemonade and set it aside. "That's a lot to deal with. Your mother is a strong person."

David's smile held no humor. "What goes around, comes around," he quoted. "Dad's third wife is the same age as me. True to his pattern, he probably started seeing her before he left Zane's mother, too."

"Has Stephanie remarried?"

David shrugged. "Who knows?" He was about to ask whether Kim's sympathy stemmed from having a straying husband of her own. Before he could, she glanced past him with a polite expression.

"Oh my God!" squealed a vaguely familiar female voice, nearly knocking out his hearing. "Are you two an item again after all this time?"

Did everyone who had seen them together today assume the two of them were dating?

He reached for Kim's hand, giving her a play-along-with-me wink, and tried his best to look like a man in love as he turned to greet whoever was connected to the high-pitched voice from their past.

Chapter Seven

"Coralee has put on a little weight since our freshman year," Kim said conversationally as David drove back down the straight, flat road to the ranch.

In the back seat, Cheyenne and Jake had finally crashed after their big day at the fair. They were both asleep and therefore—Kim thought with a sigh of relief—mercifully quiet.

"You're being excessively kind," David replied. "I never cared for Coralee in high school, and I can't say that running into her again was the highlight of my day."

Kim couldn't resist teasing him a little. "If you'd only tried out that bungie drop like I suggested, you might have come away with a genuine memory to treasure once you're too old to experience that kind of excitement anymore."

David slanted her a look. "I'm too old for it now."

"Why didn't you like Coralee?" she asked curiously. "She was certainly pretty enough back in school, with all that silvery-blond hair and those, um, curves. And didn't she make the cheerleading squad after I moved away?" Today Coralee's hair looked brittle and brassy. Her skin was coarse and she had a hard expression in her eyes.

He glanced in the rearview mirror. "She was excessively popular with a number of the football players, if you know what I mean."

"A number between two and ten?" This was a bit of gossip that Kim hadn't heard before. By the time she'd come back to visit, Coralee had moved on.

"Closer to ten than two."

"Ah." Had he been a part of the other woman's fan club?

"But not with me," he added. "Oh, no. Never with me."

"Did I ask?" Kim's tone was sharp.

His smirk was darned irritating. "You were wondering."

"If you say so." It wasn't as though she was jealous. "It could have been just a nasty rumor," she said, trying to be fair.

"Trust me, the girl had a reputation for a reason."

"Was that why you grabbed my hand like a lifeline when you saw her today?" Kim asked.

"She doesn't like you very much," David replied.

"You noticed?" So the other woman's animosity hadn't been merely Kim's imagination.

After Coralee had made a couple of pointed remarks, she'd stared at Kim's hand, still enfolded in

David's, and asked sweetly if her fancy attorney husband had come with her this time. Luckily Jake and Chey had shown up right then, saving Kim from the necessity of a reply.

"Hard to miss that much hostility," David drawled. "I was kind of hoping for a cat fight."

Kim made a face. "You wish."

"Yeah, well, it's a guy thing, I guess." He leered over at her. "So what's the deal between you two? Jealous of her biker boyfriend?"

"Just his long hair." Kim fingered her own short locks.

"Uh-huh. Now answer my other question."

"Well, when Coralee was growing up, her dad worked as a clerk at the hardware store," Kim recalled. "Big family, lots of kids, but not much money." She shrugged, wondering whether she'd ever given a passing thought to how hard it must have been for the other girl in those days. "There was talk that her dad had a drinking problem."

"So she's always been jealous of you?" he guessed. "Because you've got it all?"

"The kids from the bigger ranches and some of the townies didn't always mix that well, especially the boys. There were some drag races, a few fist fights." She slanted him a look. "Nothing like what happened to you back in California, though. No one ever got shot that I recall."

He looked annoyed, probably wishing he'd never told her why his mom dragged him out here. "I got shot *at*," he corrected her. "Lucky for me, he missed."

She closed her eyes for a moment. *Yes,* she thought. *Lucky.*

He cleared his throat. "Back to Coralee, if you wouldn't mind. Maybe today she was disappointed to see that you're still as pretty as you were in high school, while she looks as though she's done hard time. Seems to me that she didn't even graduate."

Kim was too busy absorbing his compliment to pay much attention to the rest of what had followed. Drew had accused her of letting herself go, "to embarrass him," but David said she was pretty. If he was just being nice, she didn't want to know about it.

"Do you mind if I stop by my place for a minute before I take you home?" he asked. "I need to pick up some papers for your dad."

"Sure," she agreed absently, twirling her birthstone ring. "Whatever."

As they drove down his driveway, the kids in the back seat stirred to life. Lulu came out to meet the car, barking until she recognized David behind the wheel.

"Why are we stopping at your house?" Jake asked, head popping up as David pulled in by the porch.

"I'll just be a minute," he promised.

While Kim and the kids waited, the minute stretched to five and then ten. Lulu, who had followed him inside, came back out to the porch and lay down, head resting on her paws. A cat that Kim assumed must be Calvin sat on the railing and washed its paws.

"Can we get out and run around with Lulu?" Jake asked. "It's boring just sitting here."

Kim was amazed they'd recovered from the fair so quickly. "Five minutes ago you were asleep," she exclaimed, growing concerned about David. "Go ahead and get out, if you want, but stay where I can see you, okay? We'll be leaving any minute now."

If he didn't reappear by the time she counted to fifty, perhaps she'd better make sure he hadn't slipped and cracked his head or something. Maybe he had misplaced the papers he wanted.

Her hand was on the car door handle when she saw him come back outside. He was empty-handed, and one look at his pale face and set expression told Kim that something was wrong. Immediately, she thought first of her father, and then his mother.

"Come on, kids, get in the car." His voice was flat, his mouth a grim line. "We're leaving."

"Can I use your bathroom?" Jake asked.

David shook his head. He'd taken off his baseball cap and his dark hair was standing on end, as though he'd run his hands through it. "Can't you wait till you get home?"

"I guess." Pouting, Jake got into the car and thumped against the back seat with his arms folded, but Chey leaned forward and stared up at David through the open window.

"What's the matter?" she asked with a tremor in her voice.

He dragged up a smile that was meant to be reassuring, but Kim could see the effort behind it.

"Do you want me to drive them home?" she asked as he got behind the wheel. "I can return the favor and bring your truck back later."

"No. I'm okay."

She knew there was no point in plying him with any more questions until they reached the main house, but she kept sneaking glances at his profile, concern a tight ball in her stomach. Surely he would have tried to prepare them if something was wrong with the family, rather than letting them walk into it.

During the short drive, he gripped the wheel so tightly that his hands were as white as bone. "Damn!" he exclaimed suddenly, slapping the wheel and making her jump. "I forgot all about the papers that I stopped for in the first place."

Kim put a hand on his arm. "If Daddy needs them tonight, I'll come back over later." Until she found out what was wrong, she had no idea how to help.

Rory was watering the hanging baskets on her front porch when they drove by. She waved, but David didn't even slow down.

As soon as he pulled into the driveway at the main house instead of driving the car on around back to park it, Jake and Chey got out.

"Thanks for taking us today." Cheyenne hugged the fuzzy pink stuffed pig David had won for her at one of the booths.

"Yeah, thanks. I had fun." Holding up the commando watch strapped to his wrist, Jake hesitated. "Are you coming?" he asked Kim.

"In a minute. Go on ahead, okay?"

As soon as the kids disappeared inside the house, she gripped David's wrist. He stared vacantly through the windshield as if he'd forgotten all about her.

"Do you want to come in, too?" she asked.

He shook his head mutely.

"What's going on?" If he wanted her to mind her own business, he could tell her so, but she wasn't getting out of the car until she could reasonably believe that he was going to be all right.

"I found a message on my machine at home." His voice sounded as though it had been scraped raw with sandpaper, his jaw set. "There was a car accident in Malibu this morning." He swallowed hard. "Dad's dead. So is Stephanie."

"Stephanie!" Kim echoed, confused. "I thought your father had remarried again."

Finally David turned to her. He was dry-eyed, but he looked as though he had been slapped in the head with a riding crop.

"There was a message from one of his business associates on my phone, so I called him back on his cell. That was why I took so long in the house." He sucked in an audible breath.

"He explained to me that Dad and Jennifer have been going through a rough patch, and that he's been seeing Stephanie on the side for a couple of months now." David tipped back his head, eyes shut, and pinched the bridge of his nose while Kim tried to absorb what he had just said.

She didn't know what to say, but she remembered how much his father's callous indifference had hurt David that first summer.

"Can you believe it?" His voice was bitter. "A jackal doesn't change its habits, I guess. He was cheating on wife number three with wife number two! You'd need a score card to keep track of his women." David buried his face in the crook of his arm and drew in a shaky breath.

Kim wanted desperately to comfort him, but what could anyone say in this kind of situation?

"May he burn in hell," David whispered.

Kim squeezed his hand tightly. "Don't say that. He's still—I mean was still—your father."

David lifted his head and glared at her. "I am nothing like him."

"Of course you're not!" she exclaimed. "No one would ever, ever compare you."

Had David been worried that his father might have passed on some of the very same character flaws that David resented so much? Was that why he was still single?

"Your mom raised you to be a kind and caring person," she insisted. "Just like she is."

"My mom!" he echoed, groaning. "Oh, man. I have to tell her." He grabbed handfuls of his hair and tugged. "Damn," he muttered again.

"What about your half brother?" Kim was almost afraid to ask. "Was he in the car with them?"

"No, thank God. He's fine. That's one reason Jerome called, besides wanting me to hear the news from him, of course. He's wondering what to do about Zane."

"What do you mean?" Kim asked. "Where's the boy now?"

"Jerome's got him. I don't know the details, but Jerome is leaving for Europe on business after the—" David's voice hitched "—after the funeral."

"Zane must have relatives who can take him." Stephanie was still a young woman. She would have family somewhere who would be responsible.

"Oh, yeah," David replied. "The boy has a relative, all right. Me."

David's mind was spinning like a hamster in an exercise wheel as he followed Kim into the main house. What was the best way to break the news to his mom that her ex-husband was dead? How would she take it? Would she grieve?

And then there was Zane, poor kid. Jerome expected David to bring him back to Waterloo with him. If there was any red tape involved, Jerome would certainly know how to cut through it.

But what was David supposed to do with a ten-year-old kid he barely knew? He didn't have a clue where to start.

Once they were inside the house, Kim surprised him by taking his hand. Her warm grip helped him to focus on what he had to do first. Break the news to his mother.

He met Kim's concerned gaze with a smile that felt stiff. "I'm okay." The words were automatic, disconnected. His voice sounded remote to his own ears, as though it had been electronically altered.

"No, you're not okay. You're in shock," she contradicted. "But everything will work out. You'll see." She patted his hand. "You've got family here, and everyone will help."

"She's right, son." Adam appeared in the hallway. "Whatever's going on, we're with you."

The kids must have sounded the alarm, because David's mother appeared, too, wiping her hands on a kitchen towel. She smiled at Kim and gave David a hug.

"Come in and sit down." She led the way to the living room. Settling onto the cream leather couch, she patted the cushion beside her. "Tell us what's wrong."

Kim hovered in the doorway. "I'll give you all some privacy, but I'll be in my room if you should need me."

"No, don't go!" David exclaimed when he saw her head for the stairs. He was still dealing with her comment to him about family.

Kim, who had seemed to resent his place within it so much had recognized his need and made a point to welcome him.

"Please stay." His throat felt raw, so he swallowed hard. Knees a little shaky, he dropped down beside his mother on the couch and took her hands in his. He could see the fear flare up in her eyes, and he knew there was no point in drawing out the news.

"It's Dad," he said. "There was a car accident in Malibu this morning. He didn't survive it."

She blinked, frowning slightly, and he could see her taking in the meaning of what he had said. "Stuart is dead?"

David nodded. "He was with Stephanie. She's gone, too."

"Don't you mean—oh, what was the other poor girl's name? The current wife," his mother asked with a helpless gesture.

"Jennifer," David supplied.

"She was the one with him?"

He rubbed his forehead as fresh resentment toward his father rose up and mingled with guilt for feeling this way when he should be mourning.

"No, it was Stephanie. Jerome was definite about that." David didn't figure this was the time for salacious details about their relationship, even though Jerome had told him they had spent the previous night together in a little inn. Jennifer thought he was on a business trip.

"Zane is with Jerome Field, one of dad's golfing

buddies. Jerome wants me to bring him back here after the funeral.''

''Oh, my goodness.'' His mother slumped back against the couch cushions, cheeks flushed. ''Of course. That poor little boy has lost both his parents, hasn't he? How awful.''

David felt a burst of pride that she could put aside so quickly her own feelings. Even though David found it difficult to drag up any sympathy for Stephanie, his mother was too good a person to transfer any lingering resentment she might feel onto a ten-year-old. He hoped that stealing Stuart back from Jennifer had been worth the ultimate price Stephanie ended up paying.

Adam had left the room, and now he came back with a glass of water that he handed to David.

''Thanks.'' He drank thirstily as Adam's hand touched his shoulder. He blinked hard a couple of times, reality setting in, and he clenched his teeth against the sudden rush of emotion.

He had to be strong for his mother, because knowing he was in pain would only hurt her more, as well. She'd been through enough after the divorce. Self doubts, for sure. Guilt and blame and second thoughts about her decision to leave L.A. and bring David here. He certainly hadn't made any of it easier, blaming her for everything the way he had, so the least he could do was not burden her now.

''I'm okay,'' he insisted. The words were becoming his mantra. If he said them enough, perhaps they would magically become true. ''What about you, Mom? Despite everything, this has to be a shock.''

Her gaze slid to her husband, seated in a nearby chair.

"Don't apologize for your feelings," Adam said calmly, getting up and coming over to her. "You were married to the man. You loved him and you hated him. Whatever you're feeling now has got to be pretty normal, given the circumstances."

He smiled at David, then squatted down in front of his wife. He rested his big, dark hands on her bare knees. "You bore Stuart a son," he continued gently. "I don't expect you to be indifferent about his death."

He glanced at David. "It's got to be a hell of a blow for you both."

His mother touched Adam's cheek. A look of understanding, of perfect communication, flowed silently between the two of them.

David felt a sharp pain, a jab of longing that had nothing to do with what was going on right now. He envied them the connection they had with each other, and he wondered whether he would ever find anything remotely as satisfying for himself.

He glanced at Kim, who was watching him with a serious expression. When their gazes met, her nod brimmed with understanding.

"I'm going out to the coast with you," his mother announced. "When is the service going to be held?"

"I'm not sure, but Jerome promised to let me know." He hadn't thought that far ahead. "You don't have to deal with it if you don't want to. Jennifer will probably be there. so it could get messy."

Would she bother to show up? Stuart had been with another woman when he died. God, it was all so complicated.

"I can handle seeing your father's third wife," his mother replied with a wry smile. "She's not the one he left me for. Just, God help me, don't ask me to go to Stephanie's funeral.''

Closing her eyes, she tipped back her head. ''Did she deserve for this to happen?'' she asked no one in particular. ''I certainly didn't care for the woman, but she has a child. I never, not once, wished her dead.''

''I know, Mom,'' David murmured, patting her shoulder.

''If you go, I go.'' Adam smiled and squeezed her knee. ''I can supply hankies to each of you.''

She sighed, shoulders drooping. ''Thank you, dear. Not much fun for you, either, I'm afraid.''

David hadn't realized how he had dreaded facing the ordeal alone, but now relief washed over him. ''That would be great.''

''I want to go, too,'' Kim blurted. ''Um, that is, if it's okay,'' she added quickly, biting her lip.

''Yeah, sure.'' David got to his feet. ''When I hear something more, I'll let you know.''

His mother rose, too. ''I could make us all some sandwiches, if you're hungry.''

The idea of eating caused his stomach to pitch. ''No, really. I ate a lot of junk at the fair.''

It seemed days ago that he had been laughing and feeding his face. Enjoying being with Kim and the kids. Normal everyday stuff, and now this.

He shook his head, trying to clear it. ''I've got chores. I, uh, I'd better go.''

Kim blocked his way, surprising him. ''I'd like to come over for a little bit. Keep you company, if that's okay.''

He started to refuse for a hundred different reasons, but his mother was already nodding.

"That's a great idea."

Outvoted and suddenly cranky, David needed air. Needed time alone—to figure out his feelings about all of this. Damn it!

"That's not necessary. I'm fine, really." His voice rose with each word.

No one spoke. He was already at the step leading up to the entry when he realized how rude he must have sounded. Taking a deep breath, he turned to see all three of them watching him with identical concerned expressions. Waiting for him to break down. To cry, maybe.

He held up his hand, pleased to see it steady. "I appreciate everything." He looked first at Adam, then his mother and finally at Kim. "I'm going home to call Jerome and see how Zane is holding up. I'll be okay."

The mantra again. So far as he could tell, it wasn't working very well yet.

After David's departure, Kim supervised Chey's and Jake's baths, fielding their questions about David as best she could, while her dad made a couple of calls to his brothers and Emily fixed a plate of sandwiches no one touched. When Kim came downstairs to relay Chey's request to borrow her mother's bath salts, Kim's father was with her in the kitchen.

"I think I convinced both Rory and Robin that there's no need for them to rush over here tonight," he said as Emily set a sandwich in front of him. "They both said for you to have a glass of wine and get some rest."

He glanced at Kim. "They wanted to know how

David had taken the news, but he's strong. He'll sort it out.''

"Thank you, honey." Emily still sounded a little dazed.

After Kim got the okay for the bath salts and was going back up the stairs, she overheard Emily agree that the wine sounded like a good idea.

When the kids were ready for bed, Kim watched a video with them. The entire time she stared at the screen, she wondered what David was doing and what he was thinking. He was probably busy feeding his stock, but perhaps the mundane chores would bring him some comfort.

Chey and Jake wished their parents good-night, and then Kim tucked them both into bed. They were worn-out by the day's excitement, and Jake fell asleep in the middle of his prayers. Before tiptoeing from his room, Kim kissed his forehead. She figured that at his age it might be her last chance.

"Thanks for going to the fair with us," Chey said around a huge yawn when Kim joined her. "Are you going over to David's house?"

"Maybe," Kim replied. "Do you think I should?"

"He needs a hug," Chey replied wisely.

"I'll see what I can do." Kim listened to her prayers and planted a kiss on her forehead.

"Will our daddy die like David's did?" Cheyenne asked, her expression solemn.

The question snapped Kim back with the force of a hard right jab. Her breath caught and she scrambled for an answer.

"Not for years and years," she said finally. "David's father was killed in a car crash out in California. There are a lot more people there, and maybe some of them don't drive as carefully as they should.''

She was relieved that Cheyenne seemed to accept her reply. They hugged, the little girl smelling sweetly of tangerine breezes, whatever those were, and exchanged final good-nights.

After Kim tiptoed from the room, she went to the kitchen just as Emily and her father came in through the French doors.

''Both asleep,'' Kim reported.

''Thank you so much,'' Emily gave Kim a quick hug, as though she wasn't quite sure whether it would be welcome. ''That was very thoughtful of you.''

''Take care.'' Kim patted her shoulder, surprised to realize that she was happy her father was here to comfort the older woman.

A knot in Kim's stomach loosened as he bent to place a kiss on her cheek. ''We'll see you in the morning before church.''

''Sure thing,'' she replied.

Still shaken by Cheyenne's question about his mortality, she wished for a moment that she could snuggle into the protective circle of his arms. Instead she took the car key from its hook, grabbed a bottle of water from the refrigerator and let herself out.

Once she decided definitely not to go back to Seattle, she would have to buy herself some form of transportation—as well as find a job and a permanent place to live.

Oh, God. Too much to think about tonight.

She stretched out on a chaise on the deck and stared up at the stars, wondering how David was doing.

Was he staring at the night sky in a futile search for answers, or pacing aimlessly as he wrestled with childhood memories of an indifferent father? Or maybe he was trying to plan how to make room in his life for a grieving ten-year-old half brother he hardly knew.

Drinking the chilled water, she debated whether to respect his request for privacy or to invade it. To leave him to stew alone or force her company on him.

Five minutes later she cruised down the main road past his house. With his yard light on, she couldn't tell if the windows were dark, so she came back from the other direction and turned into the end of his driveway. Feeling like a stalker, she killed her headlights and the engine.

Now what? She bit her lip, briefly wishing that she smoked so that she would have something to do. Releasing her seat belt, she leaned her head back and closed her eyes.

As a teenager chafing against her father's rules, she had envied David his freedom. Emily hadn't let him run wild, but he'd been old enough for a license and he'd had a motor bike, one of the expensive gifts his father seemed to think a decent substitute for time and attention.

Did their estrangement make it easier for David to let go or more painful, since now there was no chance—however remote—of ever fixing it?

Her thoughts shifted gears, to her own parents. Once she'd gone to her mother, Christie had kept her there with helpless tears and phony guilt as long as it suited. When she'd had no more need of Kim, she had jetted off to Italy without a backward glance.

Who cared that her precious daughter, newly separated, needed *her?* Kim—

A tapping on the window next to her head startled her into sitting upright, eyes flying open. She was desperately aware that the car doors weren't locked.

Half in shadow and half in the faint glow from the yard light, David stood beside the car, frowning down at her. His shoulders were hunched and his hands were jammed into his pockets as the wind ruffled his hair.

Her window was only down a crack, so she fumbled with the button, forgetting that it didn't work with the ignition off. Frustrated, she opened the door instead of taking the time to turn the key.

"What are you doing here," he asked bluntly, "checking up on me?"

"I'm sorry," she stammered, feeling stupid. "I didn't think you'd notice the car with the lights off."

His brows rose, his grin crooked. "That's certainly a good reason to be here, because you didn't think I'd notice," he drawled. "Hey, I'll bet you could go home and park behind Adam's house where you wouldn't be found out until morning."

Lulu was with him. She was probably the culprit who had alerted him to Kim's presence.

"What a traitor to your sex you've turned out to be," Kim scolded as Lulu's stub tail began to wiggle.

"She's been spayed, which technically makes her an it, I suppose," David said.

For a moment he and Kim just looked at each other.

"So, did you want to come in?" His tone was indifferent.

"How are you doing?" She ignored the unenthu-
siastic invitation.

He scratched his chin while he pondered her question. "I've been trying to think of everything I'll
have to take care of when I bring Zane home. I need
to clean out a bedroom for him and buy him a bed
to sleep in. I'll have to get him enrolled in school.
There's day care and clothes and dental records to
think about." He shook his head. "How do people
manage it all?"

Kim didn't think he expected a reply, at least not
from her. "It will all work out," she said with false
heartiness. "Don't be nervous about the responsibility. You'll handle it."

He sighed. "I suppose."

"Want to get in and sit for a bit?" she asked,
reluctant to leave him standing out here in the dark
with only an ugly dog for company.

He hesitated, glancing toward the house as though
he were looking for an excuse to refuse.

His reluctance stung her. "What's the matter? Got
a cake in the oven?" It wasn't as though she had
suggested they run off together. Not this time around,
like before.

He walked to the passenger side and opened the
door.

"Go on back to the house," he told Lulu.

"Does she understand?" Kim asked as the dog
disappeared into the night.

David settled into the passenger seat, knees bent.
"Seems to know my tone, probably guesses the
rest."

Kim turned the key in the ignition so he could

move the seat back, then lowered both windows to let in the air.

"I'm sorry about your father," she said, feeling helpless.

He bowed his head and closed his eyes. "It doesn't seem real yet."

"What happened that you finally gave up on him?" she asked daringly. "Did he do something, or were you just tired of trying?"

He rubbed his temples with the tips of his fingers. Was he considering his answer carefully or just measuring how much he wanted to reveal?

"You don't have to talk about it if you don't want to," she added, retreating. Maybe now wasn't the time to bring up whatever guilt or regrets he was feeling.

She guessed he wasn't going to answer at all.

"Mom used to make excuses for him all the time," he said. "'Your father had to work' or 'there was a meeting' or 'you know that he wanted to be there, but something came up at the last minute.'"

His tone was bitter. "I always figured, deep down, that it had to be my fault. I embarrassed him or disappointed him, or he just didn't like me much."

She started to protest, but he held up his hand. "Dad's indifference, his arguments with Mom, their fights, her tears, the divorce, our moving out here," he continued, ticking each new thing off on his fingers, "on some level I took the blame for the whole shebang."

Lightly he tapped his forehead again. "I wanted to believe Mom when she gave me the standard spiel about their arguing, that it wasn't my fault, they wanted different things, they had grown apart. Yadda, yadda.''

He thumped his fist against his chest. ''But in here, I didn't buy a word she said.'' He swallowed hard. ''If I had only tried harder, been smarter, more talented, obeyed the rules, we would have had the kind of family you saw on television. The smiling mom in the apron and the dad who came home every night with a briefcase and kissed her cheek. After dinner he played ball with his kid in the backyard, and he never got mad when the kid missed a catch.''

''I think that was the *Brady Bunch* you just described,'' Kim said dryly. ''Second marriage for both, if I remember right, blended family.''

David lifted his eyebrows. ''So which perfect daughter were you, Jan or Cindy?''

''I'm not perfect, and you're certainly no Greg Brady,'' she replied with a grin before she sobered again. ''You do understand that nothing you did or didn't do would have affected someone like your father, don't you? No more than there was anything your mom could have done to keep him from, uh, straying?''

He leaned back with a sigh. ''It probably sounds nuts, but I'm still working on that theory.''

She patted his hand, feeling incredibly wise. ''That's a start.''

He captured her hand in his firm grip. ''So tell me,'' he asked with a crooked grin. ''If I *was* Greg Brady, would you let me kiss you?''

David saw her stiffen. He hadn't intended to blurt the question aloud. Holding his breath, he waited for her to laugh or snarl or maybe slap him silly.

She leaned toward him, eyes gooey with sympathy. "I guess I could manage a brother-sister smooch."

He shifted, facing her squarely, and lifted his free hand to the back of her head.

"Greg and Jan weren't really related," he whispered, heart banging like a drum, "and neither are we."

Chapter Eight

Kim didn't analyze the wisdom in letting David kiss her. She didn't think at all.

His gaze, dark with need, fired her blood as he leaned closer in the dim light. Her response, tamped down for too long, climbed right up her throat as she turned her body and met him halfway. She stabbed her fingers through his hair as his hands clamped her shoulders and he yanked her to him. The feel of his hot, sweet mouth on hers banished her memories of fumbling teenage kisses.

Their knees bumped. She heard his elbow whack something hard. Her neck was angled awkwardly. Passion was no match for the cramped reality of bucket seats and an intrusive steering wheel.

He lifted his head and she opened her eyes, hiding her dazed reaction as best she could as she tried to read him. He gulped in a breath. Pleased by that small sign, she forced herself not to pant. He peeled his fingers from her shoulders and she released her vine-like grip on his neck.

"Making out in a car is damned awkward," he growled, straightening. "Some things don't change."

Her warm little glow turned cool. She wanted to remind him that he had never kissed *her* in a car, but disappointment blocked her throat. Why had she thought he might remember the details? He must have locked lips—and more—with a hundred girls since high school.

"Kim?" he asked. "You okay?"

"Of course." She was pleased that her voice was steady, unlike her tap-dancing pulse, as she gazed unseeing through the windshield "But this was a mistake, all around bad timing." Might as well get the words out before he could.

She waited, breathless, for him to contradict her.

"You're right." He scrubbed his hand over his face. "Chalk my poor judgment up to everything that's happened today, okay?"

"Sure." She sucked in the hurt, her insides clenching like a fist around her disappointment. What was wrong with her? She'd come over to comfort him. She needed to get out of here, to regroup and to figure out how she really felt about what had just happened. Especially since it was painfully clear that David's only reaction was mild regret.

Despite her own churning emotions, she reminded herself that he'd just lost his father.

"I'd better go," she said softly. Her hand reached up without her permission to touch his cheek, but she managed to turn the caress into a brisk little pat instead. "I'm sorry. Try to get some rest." Perhaps he would blame her husky tone on sympathy, as it should be.

He opened the car door, making his escape. "About the funeral..." he began.

She tightened her hands on the steering wheel, waiting for him to tell her he really didn't want her there after all.

"...I'll keep you posted," he finished. "Thanks for coming over."

She released her death grip on the wheel and started the engine as he shut his door and walked around the front of the car.

She lowered her window to say goodbye.

"Lock your doors," he said gruffly, hands jammed in his pockets. "I know it's not far, but it's late and the main road's deserted. No point in taking chances."

She pushed down the button with a flourish. "Anything else, boss?"

He didn't return her smile. "About earlier," he began, looking uncomfortable.

She made a careless gesture. "It's not like tonight was the first time your tongue's been in my mouth."

His wince pleased her.

"I just don't recall us getting it on together in a car before." Let him think *she* was the one who couldn't remember. "Anyway, don't make a big deal out of it, okay?"

If her voice was a little sharper than she'd intended, perhaps he would assume she was tired.

"Yeah, you're right. Well, thanks for going to the fair with us."

She'd nearly forgotten. It didn't seem real that it was today and not a week ago.

"I should be thanking you," she said. "You were the one who insisted on paying for everything."

His somber expression relaxed into a grin that made something hitch in her chest. "You helped me with the kids, worth every penny."

With a last wave, she raised the window and switched on the headlights. They both needed some rest, and her pride had taken enough of a beating for one night. Not only did he regret kissing her, but he'd invited her to the fair as a baby-sitter.

What had she thought, that it was a date?

She swung onto the main road and pressed her foot down on the gas pedal. David had been right about one thing, she figured with a toss of her head. The kiss was a big fat mistake, one she had no intention of making again anytime soon.

There were two reasons why he would never forget the day before yesterday, David thought grimly as he sat next to his mother, Adam and Kim in the family section of the Beverly Hills cathedral. His father had died and he'd kissed Kim.

His feelings about both events were still muddled.

A surprising number of people had gathered here to bid Stuart Major a final farewell, but in his heart David had done that a long time ago. Except for a few familiar faces and a couple of minor celebrities, most of the people seated in the rows behind him were strangers.

Under the circumstances, the absence of his father's widow wasn't a big surprise. Jerome Field had nodded to David when he arrived with his wife, both wearing black, but Zane's head stayed down as they guided him into a pew across the aisle. He was pale and his eyes looked puffy.

"Poor little lamb," David's mother crooned from beside him, under cover of the organ music. "How awful to lose both parents at his age."

Her comment reminded David that he hadn't thought of Zane's loss from the viewpoint of a ten-year-old. Right then he made a silent vow to do his best by the boy, not for their father or for Stephanie, but for the bond of blood he and Zane shared.

"Will it be hard for you to have him around?" he'd asked his mother.

She had given him the look that mothers reserve for children who disappoint them. "Is that what you think? That I could blame an innocent little boy for his parents' sins?"

"Of course not," he'd muttered sheepishly.

Sitting in this grand place while the impressive silver-haired minister prayed for his father carried with it a certain irony for David. Except for one Christmas pageant with him as a Wise Man in a robe his mom made and a fake beard that kept falling off, his father rarely came to church with them. It conflicted with his tee-off time.

David let out a sigh of relief when the service finally ended, the minister's sonorous voice, the occasional cough or restless rustle of clothing and the solemn hymns a blur of sound that ran together.

The family exited through a side door to a courtyard with a sparkling fountain and a border of tasteful greenery. After a glance to make sure that Jerome was bringing Zane, David followed Adam across the old red bricks into the sunshine that seemed too bright for a day of mourning.

His mother and Kim, both elegant in black, were already walking over to the darkly gleaming cars waiting to transport them to the cemetery.

"Holding up okay?" Adam asked as David pulled sunglasses from the pocket of his suit coat. Good thing he'd already bought it to wear to a wedding last year or he'd be here in jeans and a denim barn jacket. Or something off the rack showing too much ankle and a jacket straining across the back.

"I'm fine." He slipped on the glasses, more as camouflage than to shield his eyes, and glanced at the approaching mob. Many of them had gone out the main doors and circled around the side of the building to pay their respects.

"Nice turnout." Adam stood with him, shoulder to shoulder, as though facing down stampeding cattle. "Know anyone?"

"A few," David replied. "Here comes my half brother with one of Dad's many dear friends." He greeted Jerome, met his wife and introduced them all to Adam.

"I'm so sorry," Jerome said, classy in pinstripes and gray at his temples as he clasped David's hand.

Jerome's wife, years younger, leaned forward to kiss his cheek and show him her neckline, her perfume swirling around him with the potency of a spell. The rocks in her ears matched the one that flashed on her hand. Second wife or maybe third. David managed a perfunctory nod before he turned his attention to the little boy half-hidden behind Jerome.

After one sneaking sideways glance, Zane stared at the ground with apparent fascination. Jerome caught David's eye and shook his head slowly, expression somber, his hand resting on the boy's hunched shoulder.

"Thank you," David mouthed silently over Zane's head, hoping Jerome would understand.

Then he squatted down so that he was eye level with Zane, who looked like a miniature CEO in his sharp little suit and tie, his hair slicked down. Only his shoes, the latest athletic gear for kids, revealed his youth.

David wished they knew each other better. The dynamics of their broken family had made a relationship difficult, but not impossible. He could have tried harder.

"How you holding up?"

Zane's blue eyes were wary when he looked up. His thin shoulders lifted in a shrug. "Okay." His voice quavered.

"You don't have to worry about anything," David said. He got the words out as fast as he could, as though they would make it all fine again. "I'm taking you back to Colorado with me."

"No!" Zane cried, jerking back. His arm wrapped around Jerome's pant leg. "You can't make me go!"

Heads turned, all except those of the people who waited nearby to offer a word or two of condolence. They looked anywhere but at David and the child who dared to make a scene.

David rocked back on his heels, dismayed by the vehemence of Zane's protest. He looked to Jerome for help.

"Didn't you tell him?" David asked, as Zane ducked completely behind his father's friend, still clinging.

Jerome had agreed on the phone that Zane needed

to know right away, so he wouldn't feel unwanted or abandoned, but now the man's sheepish expression was all the answer David needed.

"There wasn't ever a good time," Jerome explained, voice a borderline whine. "It's been difficult."

David straightened, swearing under his breath as Jerome's wife leaned forward. "It's not like we're related to him," she protested. "We kept him for you for three whole days."

"Shut up, Angela," Jerome snapped, as Zane seemed to cringe.

How to make a kid feel wanted. "It was no trouble, really." Jerome swiveled, trying to pull Zane back in front of him like one pried a cat loose from a couch cushion.

"Yeah, thanks." David felt worn out. He'd actually envisioned the kid throwing himself into his arms, pouring out his tearful thanks for being rescued.

From what, the orphanage?

Zane was crying soundlessly, tears running down his face. David wanted to hug him, but the poor kid would probably freak.

He shoved his hands into the pockets of his slacks, trying to figure out what to do to smooth over the situation. Before he came up with anything, the boy's head whipped around and his anguish dissolved into an expression of sheer relief.

"Aunt Susan!" he cried, breaking his death grip on Jerome. "Aunt Susan! You came!"

David turned to watch the boy dart through the clusters of people to a plump woman in an ill-fitting black dress and matching pumps. With her was a balding man wearing a tweed sport coat and tan slacks. She looked familiar and yet David didn't know her.

"That must be Stephanie's sister from Oregon," Jerome said with a sniff as the woman gave Zane a hug. "I notified her about the service, but I didn't expect her to show up."

David glanced over at his mother, grateful that Kim was keeping her company. A man in a black suit approached him, a prayer book in one hand and a small clipboard in the other.

"It's nearing time to leave for the cemetery," he said into David's ear, as though it were a secret. "I'm so sorry to rush you, but Reverend Moore has a wedding this afternoon and he'd like to stay on schedule."

"In a minute." David barely glanced at the man.

The couple from Oregon were bringing Zane back over to him. Aunt Susan had to be related to Stephanie. That explained the resemblance.

"I'm Stephanie's cousin, Susan Beamer, and this is my husband, Mike," she said with a sad smile. "Of course you're David."

He dragged his hand from his pocket and went through the motions of a civilized male. "I'm sorry about your cousin."

She nodded, her eyes filling with fresh tears. "Thank you." She glanced around at the cars. "Could we meet later today? I know you have to go now." She glanced down at Zane, who was clinging to her husband as though he expected to be dragged off somewhere scary. Somewhere like Colorado, David realized grimly.

"We need to talk," she added quietly.

"Sure," he replied, puzzled. What could they have to say to each other beyond the usual courtesies? "About what?"

She glanced at Mike. "Come on, buddy," he said to Zane, as though he'd been cued. "Let's go look at the fountain."

Impatiently David watched them walk away. It was damned hot standing here in the sun in his navy blue suit, but he swallowed his annoyance. Obviously, Zane was more fond of her and Mike than he was of his big brother.

Whose fault was that?

Susan cleared her throat and David realized she was nervous. Was she looking for money from whatever his father might have left Stephanie?

Not only did it seem a little quick for that, but David sure as hell wasn't the one to ask. Maybe all she wanted was the name of the attorney.

"There's no easy way to put this, so I'll just come out with it, okay?" She darted a glance over at her husband, standing with Zane.

David jangled the change in the pocket of his slacks and silently urged her to get on with it.

"Did you know that Stephanie's will named Mike and me as Zane's guardians if anything happened to her?" she asked.

David stared, dimly aware that Adam had walked up to stand beside him.

"Everything okay here?" Adam asked with a nod to Susan. "The funeral director's going to have a stroke if we don't head out pretty quick."

Once again David went through the introductions.

"Let's ride together," he told Susan, making a snap decision. "You're right about us needing to talk.'' He glanced at Adam. ''Do you mind taking care of the women?''

''Taking care of the women is one of my favorite jobs,'' Adam replied, but his grin didn't mask the concern in his eyes.

''I don't see why David took the other car,'' Kim grumbled as she stared outside through the tinted window.

All the fancy homes they drove past were set back from the street, many of them screened for privacy, but she had seen newer and nicer bordering Lake Washington on the outskirts of Seattle. In her opinion, the fabulous multimillionaire estates in Medina and Hunts Point dwarfed anything Beverly Hills could offer, and the air was cleaner.

After she and their folks had come all this way to keep David company, he ended up riding to the cemetery with someone else. Kim had seen Zane at the church, but she hadn't yet met him.

''Take it easy on him,'' her father said. ''Something's going on, but I'm sure he'll fill us in as soon as he can.''

''Who was that couple?'' Emily asked. ''Zane certainly seemed to know them.'' They'd all heard the little boy's shouted protest and seen him throw himself at the woman David rode with in the other limo.

Except for thanking Kim for keeping her company, Emily hadn't said much while the two of them waited for the procession to begin. Attending her ex-husband's funeral had to be an uncomfortable experience for her, especially since their divorce was anything but amicable.

No wonder his current wife hadn't bothered to

show. Poor David, having such a jerk for a father. No wonder he'd glommed on to hers like a life ring. Sharing wasn't really so bad.

The ringing of a cell phone distracted her. With an apologetic glance, Emily dug it out of her black purse and took the call.

"Gotta stay connected when you've got kids at home," Kim's father muttered as he watched his wife's expression shift from polite inquiry to a frown of concern.

He and Kim both remained silent until Emily was done talking and had broken the connection.

"What's up?" he asked as she handed the cell phone to him.

"I know we were planning to stay until tomorrow while David takes Zane to his mother's service," she said, "but that was Rory. Cheyenne's little fever is worse, plus she's been throwing up."

Kim's father reached over to pat her hand. "Kids get these bugs, but she'll be fine. Do you want to go home?"

"She's asking for us," she replied on a sigh, obviously torn. "Why don't you stay here, like we planned and I'll try to get a flight back this evening."

Kim's father was already shaking his head. "You go, I go," he said firmly. "Kimmie and David can manage Zane." He looked at Kim for affirmation. "Right, sweetheart?"

"Of course," she replied. "Don't worry." She smiled at Emily and poked a thumb at her father. "He's never wrong, you know," she added dryly. "Chey will be fine, but she wants her mom. Go home. I'll manage brothers big and little." Wouldn't David be thrilled to hear it?

Emily gave her a grateful smile while Kim's father got the number of the airlines in order to switch their tickets.

"I'm so glad you've come home to us," Emily whispered to Kim. "And thanks for watching over my son."

The warmth of her words brought with them a rush of mixed feelings. Keeping an eye on David had gotten a lot more complicated since Kim had kissed him.

She managed a smile as the car drove through elaborate wrought iron gates. "No problem."

"We have four children of our own," Susan said earnestly. "Zane knows them all, don't you, hon?"

She and Zane sat across from David and her husband, Mike, in the limo. They seemed like nice people, regular folks from Oregon, unlike her marriage-busting cousin, Stephanie. Zane leaned against his aunt, her plump arm circling him protectively. He stared out the window as though his future wasn't being dissected like a frog in biology class.

"I'm sure hearing that Stephanie wanted us to take him is a shock," she continued, eyes watery. "Maybe you want to wait until the will is read, but with you being in Colorado and us up in Bend, it might be easier if we could work it out now." She glanced at Zane. "Less disruptive for everyone."

David didn't know what to say. Sure, the idea of taking on a small boy had thrown him for a loop at first, but he had worked his way through acceptance and then to enthusiasm. Zane was family, a connection by blood.

Now this woman he hadn't known existed until

today was telling him she had a legal right to the boy. David was on overload.

This wasn't a puppy that had been snatched away, he reminded himself. And Susan was looking at him, expecting a coherent reply.

"What do you suggest?" he asked.

She relaxed her tense posture while Mike shifted on the seat next to David. Her smile was tinged with sadness, a reminder of her loss that made David wonder how close she and Stephanie had really been. Did she know what her cousin had put him and his mother through? If he wanted, he could make her pay for their pain, but Zane would end up paying as well, and that didn't seem fair.

"Zane knows us," she said. She didn't add *better than he knows you,* but David heard the words as clearly as if they'd been spoken aloud. "We have a big old house at the edge of town. Bend is a great place, with all kinds of things for the kids to do. There's hiking, fishing and team sports. In the wintertime, we all head up to Mount Bachelor to play in the snow and to ski."

She glanced at Zane. "Remember the last time you stayed with us? We all went snowboarding."

"Yeah, it was cool." His eyes met David's and his smile was replaced by a glare, right before he buried his face against his aunt's plump side.

"Will you be attending Stephanie's service tomorrow?" she asked David.

"I'd planned on escorting my half brother," David replied, blatantly staking his claim. "We're flying back home in the afternoon."

As the car slowed, Zane's head snapped up. "I

won't go with you. I want to live with Aunt Susan and Uncle Mike.''

She shushed him gently. ''Take it easy, okay? We'll work things out, you'll see.''

Mike leaned forward to ruffle the boy's hair in a gesture whose casual familiarity wasn't wasted on David.

''We're staying at the Pacific Crest Hotel,'' Susan told him. ''We'd like to keep Zane with us tonight, if that's okay. It will give you time to consider everything.'' She glanced at her husband, who nodded.

''That's right,'' he said, the first sound he'd uttered since they climbed into the car back at the church.

''We could talk again tomorrow after the service,'' she suggested, her tear-dampened gaze adding a silent plea. ''What do you think?''

The car came to a stop and the driver went around to hold open their door. Zane scrambled out, but Susan waited for David's answer.

He felt a headache coming on, something he rarely experienced. It had to be tension.

If he let the Beamers take Zane with them for the night, he'd have time to talk to Adam and his mom. Thank God they were here, because he needed their guidance.

''Ma'am?'' the driver asked, extending his hand.

''Okay,'' David said, ''but this is just temporary.''

''I understand. Thank you.'' She accepted the driver's assistance.

Slipping on his sunglasses, David waited for her to exit the car. Then, taking a deep breath, he prepared himself to bury his father.

* * *

"I'm so sorry," David's mother said after the graveside service had been concluded. "You know how much we want to stay. Are you really, really okay with us leaving?"

"You mean, am I jealous of an eight-year-old?" David replied, dredging up a smile. To his relief, some of the anxiety faded from his mother's expression. "Of course I am, but with Kim to chaperone me, I'm sure I'll be fine."

He gave her a bland look that she returned with edgy annoyance.

"What about Zane?" Adam asked. David had relayed the short version of the situation before they'd had a chance to break the news that they were leaving right away. "Are you still bringing him home with you?"

David shrugged. "Damned if I know. It seems awfully disruptive to drag him clear to Colorado if he's eventually going to end up in Oregon, doesn't it?"

Adam gave him a long look. "No one can decide that for you, son. You're his closer relative, so you may have the stronger claim. If you decide to pursue it, we'll find a good attorney."

"Thanks," David replied. "When are you leaving for LAX?"

"Adam was able to book a flight right away, so we have to collect our luggage and go," his mother said apologetically. "I'm sorry this has all happened so fast."

"I'm glad you'll be home for Cheyenne." David was an adult and she was just a little kid who needed them more than he did right now. "Will you call me this evening and let me know how she's doing?"

"Of course we will," Adam replied. "She's your sister, too."

* * *

"Do you want to get a drink or something?" Kim asked David as the car from the funeral home pulled up in front of their hotel.

She was hot and cranky, and she felt guilty for it. Her face was stiff from all the smiling while she stood next to him at the graveside service and listened to people tell him what a good man his father had been. At least Zane had thawed out a little, but she suspected it was only because he was happy to be with his aunt.

After the driver had dropped them off at the hotel entrance, she looked up at David expectantly. "Well?" she asked. "What do you want to do now?"

He'd removed his jacket and tie in the car, rolled up the sleeves of his white shirt and freed the top couple of buttons. With his hair falling down onto his forehead and dark smudges under his eyes, he'd never looked more attractive.

Two gorgeous women who had just exited a cab turned and stared as they walked by. Kim glared back, but David didn't seem to notice their ogling. Instead he led Kim into the coolness of the lobby, jacket tossed over his shoulder.

"I'm beat," he admitted. "Maybe I'll just go to my room and crash for a while. Why don't you go shopping or something, and then we could hook up later for dinner."

"Are you sure you'll be okay?" She wished there was something she could say to make him feel better, but she didn't know what he needed.

"I wouldn't mind getting out of this dress and these shoes," she said without thinking.

He gave her a lopsided grin, letting his gaze travel down to her feet and back up again.

Too late, she realized how her remark might have sounded. "Don't get your hopes up. It's hot and my feet hurt, that's all."

"Ah, here's the Kim we all know and love," he drawled. "You've been so nice to me today that you had me worried. I thought an alien had taken over your body."

"Better an alien than you." Instantly she wanted to bite her tongue. "I'm sorry."

He held up his hand. "No, no. Jeez, don't get all weird on me again. I needed the reality check."

His wry grin sent shivers through her. More than anything, she wanted to throw her arms around him and kiss that clever mouth. Obviously what she desperately needed after all the enforced togetherness of the last hours was a breather.

"You may be right," she said with a toss of her head. "Perhaps I'll change clothes and go check out some of the boutiques." She fluttered her eyelids, unable to resist the temptation to goad him just a little. "I've got a big fat support check from Drew just burning a hole in my bank account."

David's grin turned into a scowl of disapproval, making her feel like a witch for picking on him, today of all days. What was wrong with her?

"Good idea," he drawled, turning away. "You earned it. I'll call your room about dinner."

So much for making him feel better, she scolded herself silently, watching him stride across the lobby and disappear into the crowd of people heading for the bank of elevators.

When she'd said goodbye to her father, a sudden thought about the reason they were all here in L.A. had propelled her into his arms. Life held no guarantees. He'd stiffened, but then he had hugged her hard.

"Safe trip, Daddy," she'd muttered into his shoulder, her eyes misting.

"You, too, princess." His reply was gruff, his gaze skittering away once he let her go. "We'll see you back home."

She'd felt better for the exchange, awkward though it was, and proud of herself for hugging David's mother, too. Now she had to fulfill her promise to watch out for Emily's son.

With a sigh, Kim followed him at a much slower pace. She hadn't been kidding about her aching feet. A shower sounded like heaven, and then she'd see what the hotel's trendy shops had to offer.

Chapter Nine

When the phone in Kim's hotel room finally rang, she was standing at the window with her arms folded. She had been trying unsuccessfully to distract herself from worrying about David's mental state by studying the view of L.A.'s tall buildings. How did a person breathe here? Neither this nor the Seattle area's towering Douglas firs and fog could compete with the sapphire skies and wide-open spaces of eastern Colorado.

She crossed the room, wiggling her toes as her bare feet sank into the plush carpet, and lifted the receiver, hoping to hear David's voice.

"Hey," he said, sounding energized. "How was shopping?"

"Expensive." Some of her worry dissipated, just like that fog. "Did you get any rest?"

"Sure did, and now I'm starved. How about you?"

She pictured the two of them seated across a table at the restaurant she'd passed downstairs, with its soft music, low lighting and cream linen tablecloths. They would share a meal, some conversation, and she would regain control of her attraction to him.

"I could eat." She was eager to wear the simple dress she'd bought with matching open-toed shoes. It was perfect for the evening she'd envisioned.

"Would you mind if I called room service?" he asked.

"Room service?" she echoed, dismayed.

He must have misinterpreted the tone of her voice. "I've got a suite," he said quickly, "so we'd be comfortable." He groaned. "I meant that we won't have to sit on the bed."

"Okay," she replied. "Whatever works."

"Don't get the wrong idea," he continued on as though he hadn't heard her. "But if I had to face one more group of strangers, I'd probably go crazy."

She could feel a flush heating her cheeks. Did he think she expected him to jump her, just because they'd shared that kiss?

"I understand. It's not a problem," she insisted. "Whatever you need is fine, okay? Tomorrow I'll probably go back to picking on you, but tonight I can just be your friend."

Oh, man. Did that sound as corny to him as it had to her?

"Kim?" His voice had deepened. "Thanks."

Jeez, she had to rein it in. Who'd ever thought vulnerability in a man could be so darned sexy? "You're welcome. What's your room number?"

*   *   *

David opened the door and his eyes went wide. "Wow," he said. "Come in."

When Kim saw his faded jeans and T-shirt with CSU in dark-green lettering across the chest, she felt horribly overdressed.

"I didn't bring anything casual to wear," she explained as she walked past him into the room. "I bought this in one of the shops downstairs." Feeling slightly self-conscious, she held out her arms and spun in a circle. "It cost too much, but I was tired of black," she babbled on when he remained silent.

The simple slip of a dress was moss green and sleeveless, with skinny lace straps that matched the ivory trim around the hem. Because of the cut and the softness of the fabric, the only thing she wore beneath it was a skimpy excuse for panties.

How long had it been since she cared about a man's opinion of how she looked? And why did that man have to be David? One look at his rumpled hair and his broad chest sent her objectivity crumbling.

"Whatever you spent on that dress, it was worth every penny," he said quietly. "Want something to drink?"

She glanced at the cut-glass tumbler on the table, half filled with ice cubes and amber liquid. "Just water, thanks."

His gaze followed hers. "I figured I earned a drink, since I'm not driving tonight."

While he got her water from the small refrigerator and filled a glass with ice from the bucket, she glanced around the room. Decorated in tan and cream, with dark-green and burgundy touches, it was surprisingly attractive for a hotel room. Music played softly in the background. ''This is nice.''

''I expected Zane to be staying with me.'' He handed her the water and then he picked up his glass. ''Cheers.''

Kim studied his frown and the twist to his mouth. ''Have you decided what to do about him?''

He shrugged. ''You saw how he acted toward me. The kid's had enough trauma in his life for right now, so what choice do I have but to let Susan take him back to Oregon with her?''

''Have you talked to your father's attorney?'' she asked. ''I don't know a lot about wills and estates, but won't there be a reading or something?''

''I told him to give me a call. I'm really not interested in coming back here just to find out how my father divvied up his money, except to make sure that Zane's future is secure.'' He took another swallow of his drink and swirled the ice cubes. ''Let's order, okay? It might take a while for the food to get here.''

Kim glanced at the room service menu and handed it back to him. ''A Caesar salad, the chicken pasta and a glass of white wine would be fine.''

''Sounds good. I think I'll have that, too,'' he said.

While he called in their orders, she wandered over to the brocade couch. Kicking off her ivory sandals, she tucked one foot under her and sipped her water.

Unaware that he was being watched so closely, he stretched his free arm over his head. Elbow bent, he twisted from side to side as though he was working out the day's tension. The hem of his T-shirt rode up, baring his taut midriff above the gaping waistband of his jeans. He hadn't bothered with a belt and his feet were bare except for white socks.

Kim swallowed hard. She'd known he was in good shape, but she hadn't allowed herself to consider just what that meant in terms of how his body might look.

"It won't be long," he said. "Want me to put on my shoes?"

She realized she was staring at his feet, and took a quick sip of her water to hide her reaction. "No, it's not a problem, really. I was just thinking, a million miles away, I guess." If she were Pinocchio, her nose would have grown like a carrot on steroids.

He dropped into the chair across from her. "And what were you thinking about so determinedly?" he asked.

Kim's mind went blank. Desperately she scrambled for something to say. "Um, my grandmother," she blurted, grasping. "Has Daddy ever mentioned whether he found out anything about her disappearance?"

David looked puzzled. "I can't say that he has. Didn't she take off when he and your uncles were just kids? What made you think of her?"

Desperation, Kim thought hysterically, doing her best to look innocent. "I guess your dad and Stephanie's accident got me to thinking about family." She felt guilty for exploiting the recently departed, but David's father had, after all, cheated on Emily with Stephanie. "Anyway, Grampa Winchester died before I was born, and I've only met my maternal grandparents once." She sipped her water. "It seems so bizarre that Grandma abandoned her three children and never tried to contact them again."

"Do you think that something happened to her?" David asked. "Was a missing person report ever filed?"

Kim shook her head. "All Daddy would say was the sheriff had proof that she had left voluntarily. No one wants to talk about her. Uncle Charlie was too young and Aunt Rory said that Uncle Travis acts the same way Daddy does. I guess that after Grandma left, Grampa was pretty tough on all three of them. Maybe they blame her for that."

"Mom said once that losing his mother and then having Christie leave, too, hurt Adam a lot," David replied. He didn't bother to accuse Kim of abandoning her father, too, but he didn't have to.

She didn't know what to say. Before the silence had a chance to grow awkward, the phone rang.

"I hope that's the folks calling with a progress report on Cheyenne." He got up to answer it.

After listening for a few minutes, he gave Kim a thumbs-up and she let out a sigh of relief.

"We're about to have dinner," he said, meeting her gaze as he pointed silently at the receiver.

Catching his meaning, Kim shook her head. She didn't really want either of their parents to know she was here in his room. No point in giving them anything to speculate about.

After David said goodbye and hung up, he sat back down. "That was Adam. The doctor came out, and Chey's fever is dropping. She was glad to see them and she's been asleep ever since they said hi."

"They must be relieved," Kim replied. "Anything else going on there?"

"No. Adam assumed we had reservations somewhere. Why didn't you want to say hello?"

"You said hello for me."

"He seemed a little disappointed," David persisted.

"He'll get over it." She twisted her emerald ring around on her finger. "So their flight was okay?"

Before he had a chance to answer, there was a knock at the door.

"That's got to be our food," he said, getting to his feet.

The waiter rolled in the cart, complete with crystal goblets, domed silver covers and lavender roses in a round bowl. After he'd uncovered the dishes and opened the wine with a dramatic flourish, David signed the check.

"We'll serve ourselves," he said.

"Enjoy your dinner." The waiter's smile widened when he glanced at what David had written, so the tip must have been generous.

After he'd gone, David held out Kim's chair. "Thanks again for agreeing to eat up here." He sat down across from her and held up his wineglass. "Here's to the prettiest dinner date I've had in quite a while."

While they ate, they kept the conversation light. He caught her up on the news about some of the people they both knew; she described the beautiful scenery in the Pacific Northwest and they discovered that, unlike music, they shared similar preferences for action movies, the History Channel and nonfiction reading.

When David set down his fork and leaned back with a sigh, Kim was surprised to see that all of his pasta was gone and so was hers. Neither wanted the cheesecake, so he refilled their wineglasses and wheeled the cart out to the hallway.

She curled up on the couch, expecting David to sit in the chair he'd used earlier. Instead he joined her, leaving a couple of feet between them, and propped his feet on the coffee table.

"Man, what a day," he groaned, leaning his head back as he rubbed his hand over his face. "I feel like I've been playing in a Ping-Pong tournament."

"Want to talk about it?" she asked, sipping her wine.

"Not really. Let's take my mind off me for a while."

Kim's entire body went tense. "What do you mean?"

"Let's talk about you instead."

Flustered, she glanced away. Her hand was wrapped so tightly around the stem of her glass that she was surprised she hadn't snapped it. "I'm not very interesting."

"I disagree," he said softly. "You know, I have no idea what your life was like after you left here. Tell me about your mother."

Kim was reluctant, but if talking about herself would take his mind off the day's events, it didn't seem like too much for her to do. At least he hadn't asked about her marriage, no doubt because he just wasn't interested.

"Not too long after I went to live with her in Denver, she and the owner of the gallery where she worked had a falling out of some kind," Kim recited. She had suspected they were more than merely boss and employee, but her mother had never said anything and Kim hadn't wanted to ask.

"Why did you go with her when she left?" David probed. "Why not come back to the ranch?"

"She needed me more than Daddy did," Kim said

simply. "After all, he had your mother, but the only one my mom had to count on was me."

David frowned, as though he was trying to understand, but someone who had never lived with a person as needy as Kim's mom could never comprehend the guilt she had made Kim feel whenever she thought about leaving.

I missed you so much, baby. I thought about writing, or calling, but I just didn't want to deal with your father. How can you turn your back on me, just when we're getting to know each other again? I may not have a fancy ranch, but I'm your mother. Doesn't that count for anything? I don't have anyone else but you.

"It's hard to describe." Kim picked her words carefully, wanting to make him understand. "A lot of the time I felt as though I was the parent."

He shook his head. "And then she abandoned you for some rich old geezer. That must have been about the time your marriage was falling apart. Too bad she couldn't stick around."

The urge to defend her mother was strong, but Kim didn't want to start an argument. "I don't know how much help she would have been," she said instead. "How's your bathroom remodel coming along?"

He made a face, but he went along with the change of subject. "Looks like I'll have to completely tear out the wood vanity. The pipe under the sink leaked at one time, so the bottom of the cabinet is all rotted." He snapped his fingers. "Know anyone who'd be willing to help me pick out the new tile for the counter and some paint color?" he asked. "And the flooring, too, I guess. I'm not very good at that."

Kim saw the trap, but she stepped into it anyway. "I know a little about color. I could help you if you'd like."

His smile widened. "Really? That would be great."

Her gaze locked with his. She couldn't say what she wanted to say—that she loved his eyes, loved his smile. Loved him.

No, she hadn't meant that. Of course not. She tried to retreat from the thought, to shut the door she'd inadvertently opened and the truth behind it.

"What's wrong?" David sounded alarmed. "Don't you feel well? I hope it wasn't the chicken."

The cowardly part of her wanted, oh so badly, to grab at the excuse he'd unwittingly handed her.

"I'm fine," she lied.

"Have I told you how much I appreciate having you with me?" he asked, searching her face. "Especially since the folks had to leave."

"I wanted to be here." Her voice was husky with her newfound emotions.

David's eyes darkened as he leaned closer. To Kim's surprise, he held her chin lightly while he pressed his lips to her cheek. The warm touch and the feel of his breath against her skin sent a tremor through her that he must have felt.

"What really happened?" he asked, gaze holding hers as he released her chin.

She knew what he meant. Her scar. Without looking away, she swallowed hard. "It wasn't flying glass," she admitted.

"I didn't think so. Did your husband do it to you?"

It was so difficult to talk about, but maybe she

would feel better if she did. "After I lost the baby, we had an argument and Drew backhanded me. His ring caught my cheek."

"The bastard." David's face darkened and his hands curled into fists. "If he was here, I swear I'd beat the crap out of him." He swallowed hard. "How could he possibly blame you?"

She touched her finger to the spot on her face where David's lips had been. "He figured I had cost him his heir, but I knew the only reason he wanted a baby was to please his parents." How could she have been so wrong, to think Drew had loved her?

"You could never hurt your child." David's tone rang with conviction. Despite their long estrangement, he had more faith in her than her own husband.

"Thank you."

"What did you do then?" David asked.

"I picked myself off the floor and I walked out. The next morning I saw an attorney." Her smile trembled only slightly. "Three months later, when my divorce was final, I came home. You know the rest."

"Are you staying?" he demanded.

This time the answer was easy. "Yes."

His gaze strayed toward her stomach. "And you're okay now?" he asked. "You're all healed?"

"The doctor had no explanation for the miscarriage," she replied. "I can have more children someday." She didn't add that the doctor had told her conceiving again could be difficult.

"Then maybe I won't fly to Seattle and beat up your ex, but he sure as hell deserves a good pounding for what he did to you." David pulled her into his arms. "I'm so sorry," he whispered against her hair, "but I'm proud of you, too."

She held her breath, afraid to move lest she somehow reveal the extent of her vulnerability. Her life was already in turmoil, and he was just being kind. The last thing she needed was this attraction to him.

This is exactly what you need, whispered an insidious voice inside her head—or her heart, she wasn't sure which. *What you've always needed.*

David finally let her go.

"Sooner or later I'm sure Drew will get what's coming to him," Kim said. In the meanwhile, he would have to deal with his parents, his insufferable father and ice-cold snob of a mother. That might be punishment enough.

"Kim?" David asked, drawing her attention back to him.

"Yes?" she squeaked, throat clamping up when she saw the intensity of his expression. Was it the wine that made her head spin, or was it David? He was even more appealing to her than he had been when they were younger, her first real crush.

"Will you stay?"

"I...I—" She swallowed, wishing he had just swept her into his arms and kissed her, instead of giving her a *choice.* She'd made so many bad decisions in her life.

One corner of his mouth hitched up endearingly. "Please?"

When had Drew or anyone else ever looked at her quite this way, with such longing, such hunger? Such need?

David needed her.

"Okay," she whispered.

He squeezed his eyes shut, as though he was immensely relieved by her reply. His chest expanded on an indrawn breath.

He cupped her face in callused hands that weren't quite steady and leaned closer.

"Ever since I kissed you that last time, I've been wanting to do it again," he said roughly. "Don't make me wait any longer."

As if he understood her need to set the pace, he waited for her to close the gap remaining between them. When she did, slowly, drawing out the anticipation, his gaze shifted to her mouth. Finally she could wait no longer, so she lifted up and settled her lips against his.

His fingertips flexed along her jaw and she stiffened, but then he rubbed his mouth gently on hers. He traced her lips with his tongue and her heart dropped straight down to her toes. She pressed her palms against his chest to keep herself from falling right into him.

She expected him to deepen the kiss, but instead he nibbled his way up to her closed eyelids. First one and then the other. He kissed the tip of her nose, making her smile, and then the upturned corner of her mouth. He traced the line of her jaw with his thumbs and then he skimmed his hands down her throat.

Without thinking, she arched her back like a cat. He slipped the stretchy lace straps of her dress off her shoulders. The thin fabric of the bodice slid down, as gentle as a breeze against her skin.

She tipped back her head and David lowered his, stringing kisses along her collarbone while she buried her fingers in his short, thick hair. Her nipples tingled, hard as buttons, halting the downward slide of her bodice. David nudged the fabric with his nose, sending a fresh wave of reaction through her as it skated over the sensitized tips of her breasts.

Her breath caught and he groaned deep in his throat. With his tongue he traced a lazy circle around one bare nipple. Her fingers tightened on his scalp while heat pooled between her legs, hot and fierce. She swallowed a whimper of need.

Slowly he repeated the movement around her other nipple and then his warm breath teased the skin moistened by his tongue. Needing to torment him as he was her, she slid her hands beneath the hem of his T-shirt and skimmed them back up the sides of his torso. His skin was smooth to her touch, like hot silk, and the long muscles were firm beneath her palms.

His lips closed on her nipple, sending a shaft of reaction straight to her center. She gasped, her knees automatically pressing together—too little protection against the passionate onslaught, and way too late. In retaliation, she raked her nails lightly across his chest and rubbed the small hard nubs of his nipples with her fingertips.

Her gesture unleashed a tiger. He shifted, straddling her with his knees and pressing her against the back of the couch. One big hand was braced against the cushion beside her head. The other cupped her breast and his thumb brushed the tip as his open mouth covered hers.

Kim arched up, damp and aching. Her hands sought a hold on his wide shoulders. She returned his kiss with wild abandon, her tongue stroking his, her skirt hitched up. Together they slid down so that he lay partially on top of her, his braced elbows taking most of his weight. Her thighs were parted and the evidence of his need nudged her intimately.

She bucked, and he broke the kiss. "Damn, don't move." His voice was edged with desperate laughter. "Honey, just stay still for a second," he pleaded, chest heaving.

Her body throbbed. She burned with need.

His desire was like a drug to her. She craved more.

When he finally sucked in a deep breath and reared up over her, she watched him through her lashes. Very deliberately she stretched her arms up over her head. His gaze went to her bared breasts, his breathing audible. She arched her back and wet her lips with her tongue.

"You're killing me," he rasped, hands fisted at his sides.

"You make me feel alive." The words were torn from her. Slowly she lowered her hand to the hem of her dress, already halfway up her thighs.

David leaned closer and she thought he was going to kiss her, but instead he slid his hands under her limp body and hauled her off the couch.

"You've got ten seconds to decide whether this is what you want," he said, voice thick, "because that's how long it'll take me to get you to my bed."

Cradling Kim against his chest, he crossed the sitting area in long strides and shouldered open the door to the other room. When he tossed her gently onto the mattress, she sank into its softness. Immediately he followed her down, bracing himself with his hand and his bent knee. He looked almost angry.

"Time's up," he said. The boy she'd kissed a few times in the past had been replaced by a fully aroused mature male. He didn't frighten her because it was obvious that he was holding himself under tight control. Once again, the choice was hers.

Daringly, gaze locked on his, she wiggled backward until she was able to sit up. Then, as he watched her with a muscle flexing in his cheek, she shifted her legs to the side.

He must have thought she was going to leave, because he hung his head, eyes squeezed shut. His chest expanded and she knew he was struggling for control.

Why, though, should he have any control left, when hers was gone, sent up in flames by the heat of his touch? How odd that she could feel so helpless, and yet so powerful.

"David." She pitched her tone low, seductive.

His head snapped up. When she had his attention, she rose up to balance herself on her slightly spread knees, and slid up the hem of her dress.

He knew he'd never seen anything as sexy, as absolutely mindblowing, as Kim with that half smile on her face, eyelids heavy, while she lifted her dress. She'd better not expect him to stop now, because he had given her the chance and she hadn't taken it.

Of course, if she reconsidered, wanted him to stop, then somehow he would. Even though his brain had turned to overheated mush, his arousal to granite and his willpower to ashes.

Would she, could she be so cruel as to show him those tiny lace panties if she planned to call a halt? He couldn't move, couldn't tear his gaze away as the hem of her dress hitched higher. He'd beg, he thought as he stared helplessly at her lean stomach with its sexy little indentation. He'd bark like a dog or howl at the moon, if she asked. Her bare waist appeared next, just the right size for his hands, and then those sweet little breasts he'd already tasted, her nipples like berries.

She pulled the dress the rest of the way over her head, and he managed to get out of his T-shirt without injury. If he got any harder, he'd probably split like a—

Her hands skated back down her body and she hooked her fingertips into the band at the top of her panties.

"Oh, no, you don't," he growled, heart pounding as he lunged. "That's my job."

"Then this is mine." She reached for his jeans, her fingers dipping into the waistband to graze his skin and send more blood pounding to his groin. Damned if he didn't feel lightheaded.

Before the red haze of his barely functional brain could send a message to his mouth, begging her to slow down, she freed the snap on his jeans. Desperate now, he wrapped his arms around her and wrestled her down on the bed. Her throaty giggle clouded his senses as he rolled, pulling her atop his throbbing body.

She squirmed around to press her mouth against his bare skin. Before David quite realized it, her panties and his clothing had been peeled and stripped away.

"I don't, I can't—" he babbled, remembering his responsibilities. Cursed himself silently for not thinking ahead. "I'll have to go down to the lobby and buy—"

"No, it's okay. I'm safe, really, it's okay."

He was only human. Taking her at her word, he

rose over her, his fingers busy stroking and probing her moist, hot places.

"Oh, oh, please don't stop," she sobbed, bucking against his hand.

With that kind of green light, how could a man not hit the accelerator with everything he had?

When Kim woke up again, the second or third time since David had first taken her, or they'd taken each other, the phone was ringing. A sliver of light from the gap in the draperies pierced the gloom of his hotel room.

His bare arm reached out from beneath the tangled bedding. Mercifully, the ringing stopped. "Yeah, thanks," he muttered.

"My wake-up call."

She assumed he had to be talking to her. Funny how vulnerable one little shaft of light could make a person feel when she was naked, her body almost too limp to move.

"I'd better go," she replied. "I've got to get ready for Stephanie's service."

"Yeah, me, too." He sat up, propped against a pillow, hands behind his head. His wide chest was still bare, a love bite above his left nipple.

Kim remembered that, and more. Her face burned. All she wanted was to burrow under the covers and stay there until he'd left. Instead she sat up and swung her legs off the mattress with her back to him. Her dress was on the carpet in a sad little pool of emerald green. Her panties? Hell, let the maid have them. No way was Kim going to conduct a search— not now.

"Honey?" His voice was surprisingly tentative.

What she wanted was for him to grab her, to convince her that last night hadn't been, for him, a huge mistake.

"I'm sorry—" he began.

She spun around, yanking the sheet up to cover her nakedness. "No, don't." She swallowed hard. "We're adults. It happened, okay?"

Frowning, he opened his mouth, but she kept talking, cutting him off. Scared to death of what he might say and needing to say it first.

"You've had a lot to deal with. I know that, so I just wanted to make you feel better." It hadn't come out right, not the way she meant.

His body stiffened and his face changed, going carefully blank, so she rushed on.

"Let's get through today," she went on, the words spilling over each other. "Once we're home, we can put it all behind us."

"Is that what you want?" His eyes looked black, but it was probably just the dimness in the room.

No, no, she cried out silently. But it was what both of them needed right now. She lifted her chin and dragged up a smile, pressing her lips together hard to keep them from trembling. "It's the best thing for both of us."

For a long moment he remained still, his face rigid. Then he flipped back the covers. "Fine. I'm going to shower. Why don't I meet you downstairs? We'll have breakfast before we check out."

He stalked into the bathroom without a backward glance. She watched him go, admiring with helpless fascination the perfect symmetry of his tall male form. Last night...

She sighed as the bathroom door clicked shut behind him and she heard the water in the shower starting. With a glance at the bedside clock, she put on her hopelessly wrinkled dress and the panties she'd found in the sheets.

She had let David off the hook, hadn't she? So why did he seem more annoyed than relieved?

Chapter Ten

David was relieved that the memorial service he'd had no interest in attending was finally over. He was looking forward to tying up the loose ends with Zane and then in getting the hell out of California.

How ironic. Ten years ago, every fiber of his teenage soul had been desperate to claw his way back here, and now he couldn't wait to leave the traffic, the smog, the noise and the phony, pretentious people like the ones who had turned out yesterday. Not for a final goodbye to an old friend, but to be seen by the right people while they made a fashion statement in basic black.

He glanced at Kim as she got to her feet, wearing the same tailored dress and sassy heels as the day before. The only difference was that this morning he knew every inch of the body beneath the dress.

That knowledge was killing him.

She walked up the aisle of the funeral home without a backward glance—as if she couldn't care less whether he followed her, stayed where he was or plunged through a crack in the earth.

Damn it, how could she act this way? He had been inside her, and he had felt those tiny feminine shivers when she had let herself go completely.

They woke up this morning tangled together like a couple of vines and sharing a pillow. Then she had given him the prissy little kiss-off speech, making him feel as used as some stud-for-hire whose job had been to scratch her itch.

After David had gotten out of the shower to find the suite empty, he'd called home to check on Cheyenne. At least she was feeling a little better, but Adam had already gone out to repair a windmill on the property, so David hadn't been able to ask about work. Instead he'd had to deal with his mother's concern for the edge to his voice. Given what was going on in his life, that hadn't been difficult.

At breakfast all Kim had wanted to discuss was his decision about Zane and how it made David feel. Each time he tried to bring the subject around to what had happened the night before, she veered off in another direction.

Now he followed her from the chapel to the foyer of the funeral home, doing his best to burn flaming holes between her shoulderblades. Zane, looking pale and red-eyed, waited with Susan and Mike. The funeral director stood beside them, nodding and smiling as people walked past them on their way out the door.

The turnout for Stephanie's service had been pathetically smaller than the mob attending that of big-shot entertainment attorney Stuart Major the day before. Except for Susan's prepared statement, no one had spoken out at the brief service.

"Thank you for coming," Susan told Kim, giving her a hug as David joined them.

Kim greeted Mike and leaned down to shake hands with Zane, bringing a blush to his thin cheeks. "I'm so sorry about your mom," she told him, "but it was a very nice service. She would have been pleased."

Susan's puffy face brightened. "I thought so, too." She turned to the man standing beside her. "Mr. Radovitch did an excellent job."

The funeral director beamed. "Take as long as you want," he said magnanimously. "I'll be in my office whenever you're ready to sign the papers."

Since Stephanie had been cremated, there would be no graveside service. David assumed that her ashes would end up in Oregon with the Beamers.

As would Zane, just as soon as David made sure it was what the boy truly wanted.

"You have four children?" he asked the other couple.

Susan nodded while Mike extracted a wallet from his back pocket.

"Two boys, both older than Zane, and twin girls who are younger," she said.

Mike flipped open his wallet, dropping a couple of business cards. "Kevin is thirteen." After he'd bent to retrieve them, grunting, he pointed to a school photo. Then he flipped the page. "Cory is eleven. Stacy and Sally are nine."

"Cute kids." David rubbed the side of his jaw. "Big family."

"Always room for one more," Mike replied heartily, closing the wallet and shoving it back into his pocket. "Susan's a teacher and I'm a counselor at the high school. I coach soccer, too, so there are always kids at the house."

How could David hope to compete with a scenario like that? And would it be fair to Zane if he tried?

He swallowed hard and squatted down on his haunches so his gaze was level with that of his half brother.

"If the choice was completely up to you," David asked, "what would you say?" He had no doubt that Susan and her husband had already talked to the boy, but his instinct told him they were good people.

Zane glanced up at Susan, his face anxious. "I don't want to make anyone feel bad."

A ten-year-old should never have to make this kind of choice, especially not because he'd been orphaned by parents who put their own selfish needs ahead of their child.

"It's okay," Susan said softly. "Dave is your brother and you can trust him."

Her unexpected comment affected David in a way that nothing else had, bringing a smear of unexpected moisture to his eyes that he had to blink quickly away.

As if she somehow sensed his struggle, Kim patted his shoulder. The gesture steadied him more than any words of comfort could.

"If I go home with Aunt Susan and Uncle Mike, could I come and visit you someday?" Zane asked him. "Maybe when I'm bigger, I'd like to see your ranch."

David managed a crooked smile. "How about next

summer or maybe spring vacation? You'll be settled in by then and maybe ready for another trip. Did you know that I have horses?''

Now that the scare of actually going home with David had been lifted, Zane gave him a big grin. ''Could I ride one?''

''Sure thing.'' David got to his feet and stuck out his hand to the other couple. Mike pumped it hard. Susan ignored it, throwing her arms around him instead.

''Thank you,'' she whispered before she released him.

After the exchange of addresses and phone numbers and an open invitation for David to visit them anytime, the small group walked outside to say their final goodbyes.

David gave Zane a hug. ''Take care, little bro,'' he whispered roughly. ''Stay in touch.'' Was it his imagination or did Zane cling for an extra moment before he let go?

A few moments later he and Kim walked out to the taxi taking the two of them straight to the airport. ''You did the right thing,'' she said.

''I hope so. I guess time will tell.'' He'd made himself a promise, and he realized he was already looking forward to a possible visit from Zane.

''Thanks again,'' David told Kim as they rode out to LAX. Maybe now that this issue had been dealt with, he could focus more fully on the two of them.

The look she gave him was cool. She had retreated again. ''No problem.''

Kim rented headphones, pretending to nap on the plane back to Denver. Even though she was exhausted from maintaining a polite mask in front of David, she was too wound up to actually sleep.

How could he act as though nothing had happened between them? Even though she'd given him an out back at the hotel, she had desperately hoped he would swoop her into his arms and convince her there was more to what they had shared than a simple one-night stand. Instead he'd headed for the shower like an athlete who had just scored the winning goal.

So be it. If their lovemaking hadn't meant any more than that, she wasn't about to let on that it had only confirmed what she'd been trying to ignore since the first time she had seen him again at the Denver airport.

She loved him. Chalk up her feelings as just another one of Kim's bad choices.

When they landed, disembarked and walked up the jet way, she tried not to think about the last time she'd arrived here or everything that had happened since.

"This seems a little familiar," David commented dryly as they walked through the terminal. It was the first time he'd spoken since she donned the earphones, other than to make the briefest of necessary remarks. He, too, must be emotionally drained from the trip to the coast, even if the reasons were entirely different from hers.

"Being here together, I meant," he added when she looked at him.

"A lot has happened since then," she replied.

A muscle flexed in his jaw. "No kidding."

When Kim tore her gaze from his, the first person she spotted on the other side of the gate was her father.

"Adam!" David exclaimed. "Thanks for coming."

The two men did that hugging and backslapping dance that straight men often do when they're glad to see each other. Then her father smiled down at her, arms dangling at his sides.

"Good flight?" he asked.

"Once we finally cleared airport security, everything went okay." She wished he would hug her, too. How could she blame him for being careful, though, after all she had put him through?

Tossing caution aside, she stepped toward him. Apparently it was the sign he'd been waiting for, because he swept her into his arms, hugging her hard.

"Welcome home, Kimmie."

His words went a long way toward loosening the knot in her chest.

"How's Chey doing?" she asked, once they had let each other go.

His smile widened. "She's getting better. Today she wanted a hamburger for breakfast."

"Let's get going." David shifted the bag he was carrying. "Rowdy's been feeding my critters while I was gone, but Lulu will be pining and I want to check on the horses."

"I was by there this morning," Kim's father replied. "They looked fine."

She trailed after the two men, content to listen while they talked about the ranch and the price of beef. When they got to the car, she ducked into the back seat even though David offered to let her ride up front. She immediately leaned her head back and closed her eyes, picturing again the way her father's face had lit up when she took that small step toward him. For a little while she let her mind drift.

In the front seat the men had fallen silent. She opened her eyes to stare at the back of David's dark head, remembering how they had shared a single pillow. On the stereo, a country singer described his heartache. Choices made. Opportunities lost.

For the first time, Kim allowed herself to consider her father's dilemma ten years before, as well as her own bruised feelings. He'd been falling for Emily, but must have been aware of the problems a new romance would cause with his only child.

Thank God Kim had bolted, rather than demand he make an impossible choice. And one that no parent should ever be asked to make, she could finally admit to herself.

If he had given Emily up for her... Two broken hearts don't make a whole one.

It was only as an adult that Kim could look back and see the truth, something she should have done years ago. David had run out of time with his father, but he had gained another chance with his brother. It gave a person a lot to think about.

She must have fallen asleep, because the next thing she knew, they were going down David's driveway.

"Hey, girl, hey, Lulu," he called through the open car window at the dog running alongside the car.

"That's one homely beast," Adam said.

"At least she's glad to see me," David replied.

The breeze felt good on Kim's face. She waited quietly while he grabbed his bags and thanked her father for picking them up, and for everything else.

Finally David looked at her. "You staying back there?"

Kim opened her door. "I think I'll ride with Daddy."

Her father glanced around, and then he grinned. "I'd like that."

While she made the switch, stopping to pat Lulu's head, David stood with his arms folded across his chest.

"Thanks," he said gruffly. His gaze didn't quite meet hers. His feet were braced, as though he expected an assault. As if she planned to launch herself at him? Or make an indiscreet comment about last night?

She hesitated as Lulu danced around them, and waited for him to look at her face. They would have to find their way back to a friendship of sorts, but not just yet. For now she angled her head and gave him an aloof smile that she dredged up from the depths of her being.

"No problem," she replied. "I'm just glad it's over."

He paled. Satisfaction was ashes in her mouth as she turned her back and got into the car.

"Hey, Daddy. Let's go home."

David stood and watched the sedan until it turned onto the main road. Then he picked up his luggage and climbed the porch steps, feeling more empty inside than he had in a long, long time.

What was done, was done. His father, Zane and now Kim, all lost to him in very different ways. Nothing he could do anything about. Tired as he was, he was too restless to sleep. Tossing his bags on the bed, he changed into his work clothes and took his tool box into his half-destroyed master bath.

He'd been meaning to finish tearing out the sink cabinet, to see how far the rot had spread and how much of the floor needed replacing. Now was as good a time as any for some mindless physical labor.

When he had everything out of the cabinet, he started to pry up the bottom board. To his surprise, it lifted out easily. Funny that he'd never noticed before that it hadn't been fastened down.

Grabbing a flashlight, he peered into the cavity under the board to check out the floor. There in the opening was a flat package wrapped in a plastic bag.

Puzzled, he lifted it out of its hiding place and sat back onto his heels to open it. Inside the bag was a high school annual from nearly fifty years before and with it was a letter. When he read the name on the return address, his eyes widened with surprise.

As he pulled around behind the house, Kim's father looked over at her and smiled. She wondered whether he could see that something about her was different.

Could he tell that she had slept with David? Oh, please, not that. Obviously, she was no more able to handle a relationship with the grown man than she had been the boy of sixteen.

"Did I ever thank you for letting me come home?" she blurted out.

Her father studied her face. "Having you here is all the thanks I need." His voice was husky and his green eyes, so much like her own, were suspiciously bright as he touched the small scar on her cheekbone.

"Is there anything I should know?" he asked. "Anything you want to tell me?"

Again she thought of David, even though she figured that her father was referring to Drew and her marriage.

How she wished she could ask his advice about David *now,* but he loved David like a son. His loyalty would be divided, torn in two, just has it must have been before she left the last time. The only difference this time around was that she knew he had enough love to share.

"I'm fine," she said with a smile that wobbled only slightly. "But I could use your advice in picking out a car. Borrowing this one every time I need to go somewhere is getting kind of old."

He beamed and patted her knee. "I know someone who can help," he replied. "I'll give Denny a call and we'll put it on the ranch account."

She recognized the comment for what it was, an offer to help rather than an attempt at controlling her life.

"I'd appreciate meeting your friend and your help in getting a good deal, but I can pay for the car myself." She hoped her smile would show him that she hadn't taken offense.

"You sure?" he asked.

She nodded. "I've got a few nice pieces of jewelry that I need to sell."

"You know you don't have to do that," he protested.

"I know, but I want to. I don't care for any of it, and I'd rather have something small and red to drive than something gaudy to wear."

Her father laughed as he reached for the door handle. "That's a relief. For a minute I thought you were going to say 'something fast.'"

She got out of the car and gave him a cheeky grin across the top. "That's a given, but don't worry. I'll be okay."

"Worrying about you is my job," he replied. "But I know you'll be just fine. You're a Winchester, through and through."

He got her bags from the trunk and followed her up the steps. The door burst open before Kim could reach for the handle.

"Welcome home!" Jake shouted. Behind him was Chey in her bathrobe and then Emily, who was also smiling.

"Okay, okay, kids." Expertly Emily shepherded them aside. "Let the poor girl get in the door before you knock her down."

"It's good to be home," Kim said sincerely.

They all spent a few minutes sharing preliminary news and greetings, and then Kim excused herself to climb the stairs with her luggage.

"When you have a minute, Robin wanted you to call her at the clinic," Emily said.

Kim looked back over her shoulder. "Did she say what it was about?"

"She just asked when you'd be back. Do you need the number?"

"Thanks, I'll get it in a minute." Kim was puzzled. She liked Robin, but she didn't know Uncle Charlie's wife all that well. Maybe her aunt was looking for someone to baby-sit little Amanda.

When Kim walked into the kitchen later, Emily was putting together a pan of lasagna.

"That smells wonderful," Kim said, breathing

deeply. "Is there anything I can do after I call Aunt Robin?"

"You could throw together a salad," Emily replied as she slid the pan into the oven. "And Adam said you're going to buy a car tomorrow. Does that mean you'll be staying?"

"I thought I might give it a try." Surely she could avoid seeing too much of David, even in a town the size of Waterloo. "Don't worry, though. I've got money. As soon as I find some kind of job, I'll look for a place to rent."

Emily came around the center island, surprising Kim by grasping her shoulders. "Have I done something?" Emily demanded.

"Wh-what do you mean?" Kim stammered, a little alarmed by the intensity of her stepmother's expression.

"Have I made you feel unwelcome?" Emily released her. "If I did, I apologize, because you've a home here for as long as you want."

Realization dawned on Kim with a rush of relief. "No, no." She patted Emily's arm. "I just need to get on with my life." To Kim's surprise, moisture filled her eyes. It must be jet lag. "I hope you understand."

"Of course I do, sweetie." Emily seemed to hesitate for a moment. "After I divorced David's father and dragged him with me out here, I was determined to make my own way, too, on my own terms. Of course, I met Adam and the rest is history, but I do understand how you feel."

"What do you mean?" Kim asked, alarmed. Was she that transparent? What if Emily said something to David?

"You need your independence, and you can't get it by staying here. If there's anything I can do to help in any way, just let me know, okay?"

"Sure." Kim breathed out a sigh of relief. "Thanks."

Emily handed her a piece of paper with a phone number written on it. "Go ahead and use the phone in the office. Your dad's gone outside."

Kim went into the ranch office and sat in her father's big leather chair. Spinning it halfway around, she could remember coming in here and playing with her dolls on the braided rug while he worked on the ranch accounts.

He'd mutter under his breath and sometimes he would forget she was there and say a bad word before he caught himself. She would giggle whenever that happened, because he always got so embarrassed. Then he would lecture her about the importance of keeping her temper under control.

Now she punched in the clinic number, asked for Robin and studied the familiar plaques and pictures on the walls while she waited for her aunt to come to the phone.

As soon as Kim identified herself, Robin greeted her enthusiastically.

"My receptionist's sister in Missoula is going in for a hip replacement in three days and Erline needs to go back there," Robin said. "I wondered if it would be possible for you to fill in for a couple of weeks, just until she gets back. We don't pay much, but you'd get to meet a lot of cuddly animals and one pretty cute young vet."

Kim heard a hoot of feminine laughter in the background. Her first impulse was to make some excuse and beg off, since she hadn't worked in several years, and going into a strange situation was always difficult for her. When she had mentioned finding a job, she hadn't meant today.

"Please," Aunt Robin pleaded before Kim could answer. "The work isn't that hard. It's mostly answering the phone, taking messages and scheduling appointments."

"If I can do it, anyone can!" called out the same female voice as before.

"You heard Erline," Robin said after she'd shushed the other woman. "A monkey could do it." More laughter. "I'm really stuck, so she might not be able to go if you turn me down."

Robin was exaggerating, of course, but Kim's automatic refusal died on her lips. The job was only temporary, but it might be a good way to reacquaint herself with the locals and drum up some other leads. Finding something permanent wasn't going to be easy around here, and she hated the idea of a long commute.

"When would you want me to start?" Kim asked cautiously.

"I know you just got back from California, but if you come in tomorrow, Erline would have time to show you the ropes before she goes. I'm sure Emily would be willing to bring you by or lend you her car."

"Actually, Daddy and I are going shopping for wheels for me in the morning," Kim told her. "Could I start after lunch?"

"That would be perfect," Aunt Robin replied immediately. "Do you know where we are?"

"Doc Hanson's old place, right? I remember."

"Terrific. We'll see you right after lunch. If I'm not here, look for the woman dressed like a parrot."

After they exchanged goodbyes, Kim hung up and went back to the kitchen to make the salad. Her father came in from outside, so Kim told him and Emily about her new job.

"Sounds good," he said. "I'll call Denny tonight and let him know we'll be in. As soon as I get back from the bunkhouse in the morning, you and I can go see what he's got, if that works for you."

Kim was about to answer when the sound of a truck pulling up behind the house interrupted her. Her dad glanced out the kitchen window.

"It's David," he said. "He looks upset."

Kim was torn between curiosity, aching hunger and reluctance to see him again so soon. Curiosity and unwillingness to raise anyone's suspicion by racing upstairs won out, just as he appeared at the French doors. She braced her hands on the counter and stayed put.

"Everything okay?" Emily asked as she let her son into the kitchen. "You pulled up so fast that you raised a cloud of dust."

David was holding a book and an envelope in his hand. He wore the same faded T-shirt that he'd had on the night he and Kim had kissed in the car. Not that he would probably remember that. Paint-stained jeans with a tear in one knee hugged his narrow hips and muscular thighs, and he wore dirty white tennis shoes instead of boots. Even with a smudge of dirt on his cheek, he was still the most attractive male Kim had ever seen.

"I'm fine, Mom," he replied with a trace of impatience. "I just found out some interesting news that I wanted to share with you and Adam right away.''

My God, Kim thought on a wave of nausea. Has he met a woman? Gotten engaged? Why had she assumed that he wasn't seeing anyone, just because he'd jumped into bed with her?

Suddenly her knees felt weak and she regretted not escaping to her room when she'd had the chance.

''Kim's got news, too,'' Emily announced with a cheery smile.

David gave Kim a cursory glance, clearly uninterested. ''That's nice.''

''Where did you get the Waterloo High School annual?'' her father asked, craning his neck to look at the cover. ''Wow. That's an old one.''

''I thought about waiting until I could round up Charlie and Travis, too, but I figured that would take too long. You're the oldest, so they shouldn't mind if I tell you first,'' David continued, the words spilling out.

Kim's father looked at his watch. ''Charlie's probably at the club already and Travis went to the dentist in Kiowa. I don't know if he's back yet.''

David walked over to the dining room table and pulled out a chair. ''Where are the kids?''

''They're over at Rory's. Do you want me to call her?'' his mother asked.

He shook his head. ''No, not now. Maybe you'd better sit down. You, too, Adam.''

''What's the big deal?'' Kim asked, annoyed at his ability to ignore her so easily while images of his naked body danced in her head, just like hunky,

X-rated sugarplums. It wasn't fair! "You're certainly being dramatic."

Finally he focused on her. "It seems like a big deal to me. I think I've just discovered what happened to your grandmother, and why she left town."

Chapter Eleven

Kim's gaze flew to her father and then back to David. "You found out something about Grandma Winchester?" she echoed, puzzled. "But she left Waterloo a long time ago, when Daddy was a little kid."

"I was eleven." Her father's face had gone as hard as stone. Emily practically forced him into a chair, but he didn't appear to notice.

David's attention was riveted on him. "I found a letter that she wrote," he said. "Do you want to read it, or shall I tell you what I've pieced together from it and the inscription in this old annual?"

"A letter from my mother?" Kim had never seen her father look so forbidding, not even when she had missed her curfew. "Where was it?" he asked.

"The letter and the annual were under a panel in the master bath, in a plastic bag," David replied. "Maybe I shouldn't have read them before I came to you, but at first I didn't know what they were, and then I got curious. I'm sorry."

"It's okay." Her father sighed heavily. "Why don't you just hit the low points for us."

Emily, sitting beside him, clasped his hand between both of hers. Their obvious closeness didn't evoke in Kim the usual jealous twinge her mean little self had always felt in the past. She must be finally growing up.

"Why would something from Adam's mother be at our old house?" Emily asked. "I'm confused."

"Remember that promise you had to give Mr. Johnson when you bought his place, that you wouldn't sell to Adam even though it almost cut his land in two?" David asked her.

"I contacted Johnson's niece after his passing, to see if she would let me know if she found anything in his papers that would explain his animosity," Adam said. "She agreed, but then I didn't hear back from her. We figured the mystery died with him."

David cleared his throat and tapped the cover of the old annual. "Back in high school, Ed Johnson and Garth Winchester were both interested in Margaret Petrie, but of course we know she married your father." He hesitated. "Do you think the two of them were happy together?"

Kim's father drummed his fingers on the table. "Daddy wasn't afraid of hard work. He drove himself to build this ranch and to provide for us, but God knows he had a mean streak. He wasn't a kind man. From what I remember about my mother, she was gentle and soft spoken. She didn't stand up to him much. None of us did." He paused for a moment, but no one else spoke.

"One day when Travis and I got home from school, the old man was waiting at the house with Charlie, who was just a little tyke." He sighed, as though dredging up the past was still painful.

"Daddy told us that Mama was gone. She'd left and she wasn't coming back. Of course we both started crying and asking questions, but he said if we ever mentioned her again, we'd get a whipping." The muscles in his jaw bunched, as though he was clenching his teeth. "He kept his word on that, and we never heard from her again."

It was the most Kim had ever heard him say about his childhood. When his first wife, Kim's mother, left him, too, he would have seen it as a pattern he could never escape.

Kim's own abrupt departure must have cut him to the core. Thank God he hadn't sacrificed Emily for her.

His free hand gripped the edge of the table. Without thinking, Kim put hers on top of it and squeezed. He didn't look at her, but some of the hard lines in his face lessened.

David cleared his throat. "There's no easy way to say this." He traced the printing on the book cover with his finger. "The letter was from your mother to Ed Johnson. The envelope didn't have a return address, but there's a Sacramento postmark."

He cleared his throat. "Apparently before she left, she found out that your father had been seeing a woman over near Fondis for quite some time. Your mother argued with him about it, and then she turned to Ed for comfort."

"I feel so bad for her, even after all these years,"

Emily murmured. "It must have been a horrendous situation."

"There's more," David said. "Your father found out about Johnson. He threatened to expose him to the community and to tell you kids what your mother had done. She was afraid you'd never forgive her."

"That doesn't make any sense," Kim protested. "Grampa was playing around, too. Are you saying that she walked out on three children because she didn't want to face a bunch of gossip?"

"Things were different back then," her father reminded her. "There was still a double standard, and Daddy was a rancher with a certain amount of power in the community and at church. He could have made it hell on both of them."

"And humiliated himself by admitting that his wife had strayed," Kim retorted. "Not to mention what he'd been up to."

He shrugged. "Maybe he didn't care, or perhaps he figured on her wanting to spare her children from even more embarrassment."

"It sounds like she did try to contact you later on," David said, tapping the letter with his finger. "My guess is that your father didn't want you to know."

"Why didn't Mr. Johnson ever say anything?" Emily demanded. "Was he so bitter that he blamed you for whatever your father had done?"

"There's no way of knowing his reasons," David replied.

"My God," Kim's father whispered, his head bowed. "Maybe she did care about us."

David slid the letter across the table. "Of course she did. Read it for yourself."

Adam's hand closed over the letter. "It's a lot to take in."

Kim glanced at her watch and slid back her chair, glancing at Emily. "I'd better go pick up the kids. Don't worry, though. I won't say anything to Rory."

David, too, got to his feet. "I've got to head back, as well. I've got chores. So you'll tell Charlie and Travis?"

Her father nodded. "As soon as I can." He got to his feet and extended his hand. "Thanks."

Her mind spinning, Kim went down the hallway to the front entry. Two mysteries cleared up, just because David had decided to remodel his bathroom!

"Hey, wait up," he called from behind her.

Reluctantly she stopped.

He motioned toward the door. "Got a minute?"

"Okay." She went outside, trying to ignore the effect of his nearness on her battered senses, struggling to stay focused on the news she had just learned about her family tree.

"How do you think Adam took it?" he asked, once they were outside and he had closed the door behind them.

She frowned thoughtfully at the familiar landscape. "From the time I was little and first asked why I didn't have grandparents like the other kids, I picked up on his reluctance to talk about his childhood." She shrugged, wishing she could throw herself into David's arms and be comforted. "I figured that Grampa had been hard on them, but I never understood what they went through, losing their mama like that."

Kim couldn't stop the sudden tears from spilling down her cheeks. She turned away, hugging herself tightly. From the corner of her eye she saw David start to reach for her and she held her breath, heart hammering, but he took a step back instead.

"I'd better go."

She felt like sobbing, but instead she managed to rein in her emotions. "Thanks for coming over. We'll be fine, all of us."

"Yeah, your dad's tough, and he's got my mom to lean on." David snapped his fingers. "Oh, hey, she said you had some news, too. What's up?"

Kim had almost forgotten about her conversation with Aunt Robin. "I'll be filling in at the veterinary clinic for a couple of weeks," she said. "So Daddy and I are going car shopping in the morning."

"Well." David smiled, making her heart turn over. "Great. You'll do a fine job. Robin's lucky to get you."

His words of encouragement reminded Kim that they had been friends, sort of, before they had rolled around in the sheets together.

"How are you doing so far?" she asked. "Are you okay?"

"Yeah, I'm fine." He stood looking down at her until the silence between them grew awkward.

She would have given a great deal to know what he was thinking. "I'd better go see about the kids," she said, hoping he might offer to walk over to Rory's with her.

"Well, like I said inside, I've got chores."

"Take care." With a flip of her hand, she walked away. When she didn't hear the front door opening or closing, she finally sneaked a glance over her shoulder in time to see him disappear around the side of the house. He probably didn't want to intrude on their parents so soon after setting off the big bombshell.

A few minutes later, he drove past her, slowing so he wouldn't cover her with dust. By the time his truck turned onto the main road, she had composed herself sufficiently so that neither her aunt nor the kids would ask what was bothering her.

Working alone because two of the vets were out on calls and Todd had the day off, Kim was surprised to realize that her first week at the clinic was nearly over. Each day flew by, and yet she felt as comfortable as if she'd been working here for a year. The pace, although sometimes frenetic, was never stressful. It was a good thing, because she was a little more tired than usual even though she slept fairly well. Better than she had in Seattle, but maybe the stress of the past few months was finally catching up with her.

The young vet, Todd Cameron, was a good-natured flirt. His blatant flattery stoked Kim's ego, but his bland looks did nothing to rev her jets. It was just as well, because he'd shown her a picture of his girlfriend back home in Kansas.

While Kim smothered a yawn, one of the phone lines lit up. "Waterloo Veterinary Clinic," she recited. "How may I help you?"

It seemed that Precious needed its vaccinations updated. Kim checked the schedule on her computer screen and set up a time for old Mrs. Huber to bring the aging Persian in for its shots.

Sophie called from the Patterson spread to confirm the location of her next appointment. She was pleasant to work with, and Kim looked forward to getting to know her better.

Kim was enjoying herself. Each day she got up with a sense of purpose that overcame her fatigue, and each afternoon she left work with a pleasant hum of accomplishment.

Now she looked through the front window at her shiny new car. True to his word, her father had helped her to pick it out the morning after they found out about Grandma Winchester, and he had told her he was meeting with his brothers that afternoon to tell them about their mother.

When Kim had gotten home from work that night, something about her father was different—as though a weight he'd been carrying for a long time had finally been lifted. Over the dinner table he had reported that both Uncle Travis and Uncle Charlie read the letter from their mother and the inscription in Ed Johnson's high school annual.

"We may not agree with the choice she made at the time," her father added quietly, "but I think it helped all of us to know she didn't forget us."

Kim had felt a spurt of envy, and then she immediately berated herself for being selfish. It wasn't closure she needed with David, but a reverse love potion to help her stop loving him.

She was posting invoices to customer accounts on the computer when Aunt Robin came back from a call.

"Everything going okay?" she asked.

"It's been quiet." Kim handed her a small stack of messages.

She glanced at the first slip, from one of their suppliers. "I didn't go to veterinary school to learn how to order dog food and to inventory syringes,'' she grumbled.

To Kim's surprise, Robin didn't immediately disappear into her own office. Instead she leaned against the counter.

''So how do you like working here so far?'' she asked.

''I love it!'' Kim exclaimed. ''Too bad my two weeks are half-over.''

Idly, Aunt Robin flipped through her message slips. ''Did I mention that Erline called me this morning? Her sister has had some complications that are slowing her recovery.''

''Oh, dear.'' Kim had taken an instant liking to Erline. Her wardrobe and her outlook on life made her seem thirty years younger than Kim knew she must be, and she'd told a few stories about Robin that made the petite veterinarian blush.

''The prognosis is encouraging, but Erline would like to stay with her for a couple more months to help out.''

''Really?'' Kim folded her hands together in her lap beneath the counter, her hopes lifting.

''You've been doing a great job. I know you want to look for something permanent, but I told her I'd ask if you'd be willing to stay on until her sister is better.''

''I'd be happy to,'' Kim responded, ''but I'll have you know that I expect a dynamite letter of recommendation when I leave.''

''Deal,'' Robin said with a laugh and stuck out her hand.

Perhaps this was a sign that things were looking up, Kim thought after they'd shaken on the deal and her aunt disappeared into the supply room to inventory pet food.

A couple of weeks later, Kim wasn't so sure.

While David was in town, he stopped at the veterinary clinic to pick up a case of cat food. For once he was grateful that Calvin needed a special diet, since coming here would give David an excuse to see Kim. Ever since they'd gotten back from L.A., he hadn't been able to stop thinking about her or the night they'd spent together.

He'd lost her once. If a relationship between them wasn't meant to be, he wanted to hear it straight out. At about three o'clock this morning, he had decided to ask her to dinner tonight and find out once and for all whether he stood a chance with her.

He wiped his damp palms on his jeans and went inside, but the reception area was empty. Maybe Kim was taking a late lunch.

A cat meowed from somewhere in the back, followed by the yip of a small dog. He could hear water running in one of the other rooms with the door partly closed. Perhaps whoever was behind it could tell him how soon Kim was coming back.

As soon as the faucet shut off, David raised his hand to knock on the door.

"Why do people even have pets if they aren't going to take care of them?" he heard Kim ask. She sounded upset. "Coralee dumped that poor mama cat and her two kittens on the counter like a sack of garbage. She said she didn't care what we do with them as long as it doesn't cost her any money. What did she think would happen to an unspayed female she let run loose?"

"At least she brought them here instead of leaving them beside the road, or worse."

He recognized Robin's voice, and then a sniffle that had to be Kim. "I know." Her voice quavered, making him feel bad.

Who would have guessed that she had such a tender heart. Maybe she would take pity on him.

"Perhaps you're just identifying with Mama Cat," Robin said. "Have you seen a doctor yet?"

David froze, his hand poised to knock on the door. He shouldn't be eavesdropping like this, but if Kim was ill, he wanted to know.

What were the chances of someone walking in and catching him? The front steps were visible through the window, but he had to know what Robin meant.

The dog barked again, a series of sharp little yaps that prevented David from understanding Kim's reply. Frustrated, he glanced around and leaned closer to the door, straining to hear.

"Does your ex-husband know you're pregnant?" Robin asked.

Ex-husband? Pregnant? The words made no sense. His breath backed up in his throat and he shook his head to clear it.

"The baby isn't my ex's."

Suddenly the implication penetrated his thick skull. Kim was expecting a baby.

David had to be the father. A buzzing sound filled his head and his legs turned to water. He grabbed for the counter as the full meaning of what he'd just overheard hit him with the force of a freight train.

He hadn't used anything, because she told him not to worry. Over the roaring in his head, he heard her start to cry in earnest. Part of him wanted to slap open the door and haul her into his arms, but he didn't seem able to move.

Was she worried about another miscarriage? Was that why she hadn't let him know?

Or maybe she had no intention of telling him. But how could she keep the news a secret in a town the size of Waterloo? Hell, he needed time to think before he confronted her.

Almost tiptoeing, he sneaked back out the front door, closing it quietly behind him with a hand that shook. A baby. Nothing would ever be the same again.

Kim stared up at her aunt, tears finally stopping. Last weekend her breasts had begun to ache, but she'd thought it was part of her body's normal monthly cycle. She'd had some light spotting, too, unusual for her, but it was only after she had lost her breakfast three mornings in a row that she started to put the pieces together. A kit purchased on the sly over at the pharmacy in Elbert had confirmed her vague suspicion.

If only Robin hadn't walked into the tiny rest room as Kim was losing her lunch yesterday. If only Kim had come up with a plausible reason instead of blurting out the truth. If only she hadn't played the odds at the hotel back in L.A., assuming that the risk was infinitesimal and protection wasn't necessary. How many women had thought *that* over the centuries and been wrong?

If only David returned her feelings. *If only.*

Robin patted her shoulder. ''What can I do to help?''

Her aunt's caring expression brought fresh tears to

Kim's eyes. "I don't know." She had really screwed up this time. Perhaps she just wasn't capable of making choices that didn't turn her life upside down.

She pressed her hand to her stomach, heart soaring despite her dilemma. She was carrying David's child. After her miscarriage, the doctor warned her that the odds against conceiving again would be high, but she saw no reason that Kim couldn't carry a child to term.

"You'll figure it out." Robin got to her feet. "I'm here for you. Keep in mind the women's clinic and the support group over in Elizabeth, too. If you want, I'll give you a name and a phone number."

"I don't think I'm ready for that yet." Before she shared the news with anyone else, she owed it to David to tell him. What she hadn't yet figured out was how.

What she did know, finally, was that she was finished making the wrong choices for the wrong reasons. From now on she was taking control of her life.

After David had left the clinic, he did what he always had when he needed to think. He went home, whistled to Lulu and saddled up.

When his mother and Adam had tied the knot, Ed Johnson's twenty acres had become part of the bigger ranch. She'd bought David's first horse, an Appaloosa named Puzzle, from Adam. Just last year David had given Puzzle to a neighbor girl getting into Little Britches Rodeo.

Now David could make out a herd of Winchester cattle in the distance and two men on horseback. What he needed wasn't human companionship, it was solitude. He guided Custer in the other direction and gave the Ranger his head.

For a while the feeling of freedom was enough for both horse and rider, but eventually Custer began to tire. Lulu had dropped back, but the spotted gelding would run his heart out if David let him.

Easing back on the reins, David swung his mount around in a wide semicircle until they joined up with the dog again and all three headed back the way they had come. The fastest horse in the world couldn't outrun a man's thoughts, and David had some hard thinking to do.

As Custer slowed obediently, David leaned down to pat the horse's sweaty neck.

"Good boy. You, too, Lulu."

The dog barked sharply. Custer's ears swiveled around and his bridle jangled. The ride had cleared David's head and he'd begun to work out a plan.

"Mmm, something smells wonderful." Kim walked into the kitchen and glanced at the pair of pies cooling on the counter. Her earlier nausea had faded and now she was hungry.

"What kind?" she asked Emily as she bent down to inhale deeply.

"Blueberry." Emily was peeling potatoes for dinner. She had told Kim once that cooking relaxed her, especially after the meticulous restoration work she did in her studio. "How was your day?" she asked.

Kim felt a twinge of guilt. She was carrying Emily's grandchild, but she couldn't yet share the news. How would Emily feel about it, and Kim, when she found out?

Even more important, what would Kim's father

say? Would he be excited about his first grandchild or disappointed that she had let him down?

What she did know, without a shadow of a doubt, was that he would stand by her, as he always had—ready to help, even if she threw his offer back into his face.

"Kim? Is everything okay?" Emily watched her with a concerned expression.

"Of course," Kim replied smoothly. "I'm just a little tired, that's all."

"Oh, dear." Emily sounded disappointed as she glanced down at the pies.

"Why?" Kim asked. "What's wrong."

Emily sighed, wiping her hands on her apron. "It's just that I'm a little behind schedule with dinner, so I was hoping you'd run one of these over to David's for me." She glanced around the kitchen as though she had a dozen more things to do.

The last thing Kim wanted was to see David before figuring out what she was going to say. And yet, Emily had gone out of her way to make Kim feel welcome, so she tried to help out around here as much as possible. Perhaps David wasn't home yet, and she'd be able to leave the pie without seeing him.

"No problem." Kim managed a bright smile. "I'll leave right now."

When she saw his truck parked in front of his porch a few minutes later, she wished she'd made up some excuse. Maybe she would just pull over and eat the pie herself. She'd tell Emily she'd been mugged. *Pie-napped!*

Before Kim could give in to temptation, she clenched the wheel tighter and forced herself onward.

As she pulled up next to his red pickup, he appeared from around the other side of the shed.

For a moment she couldn't move. All she could do was stare through the window and wish there was a way to start over with him.

He came up to the car with a bridle dangling from one hand.

"Nice wheels," he said with an admiring glance. "How do you like it?"

"Daddy thinks it's too fast." She rolled her eyes.

"Yeah, he told me."

She should hand over the pie and get out of here, but she couldn't tear her gaze from his face. Once she confessed, he might never look at her again without feeling resentment or obligation. He would do the right thing, of course, but how did she know what the right thing was?

A loveless marriage? Shared custody? Or would he fight to take the baby, dividing their family in two?

While she was scaring herself with possibilities, he leaned down to her window and looked inside.

"Pretty cool." He breathed in deeply while she struggled not to bury her face in his wind-ruffled hair. "It's got that fresh-baked aroma all new cars should have," he teased.

Kim swallowed hard. "That's blueberry. Your mom sent a pie."

He straightened and reached for the door handle. "Want to come in?"

"Oh, thanks, but I've got to get right back," she babbled, panicking at the idea that she might somehow slip up, or that he might be able to tell her secret just by looking at her. As though she had somehow started to show since this morning, or had "P.G." stamped on her forehead in pastel blue and pink ink.

"I promised your mom I'd help with dinner," she lied.

A fleeting expression crossed his face, gone before she could interpret it. Disappointment or just a trick of the light?

No matter. They would have to talk very soon.

"I could come back later, after dinner," she suggested. "To see the bathroom."

"The bathroom?" He frowned, and then his expression cleared. "Oh, yeah, the remodel." He raked his hand through his hair. "I'll show you the secret compartment where Johnson hid the stuff he got from your grandma."

Was there something on his mind so pressing that he'd forgotten all about it? Another woman, perhaps? Even though she hadn't heard a whisper of gossip about him dating anyone since Kim had come back from Seattle, the idea he might was a devastating reminder that his heart didn't belong to her. As much as she might like to pretend differently, she didn't dare believe it ever would.

Chapter Twelve

He had made a lot of mistakes, David realized as he cleaned up the kitchen. Now fate had upped the ante, but if Kim suspected how he really felt, she might run screaming back to Seattle and he would lose her for good. He'd have to be careful how he reacted when she told him her news.

After she had brought over the pie earlier, he heated himself a bowl of canned beef stew in the microwave. When he sat down to eat, his appetite had fled and so he gave the stew to Lulu.

He wiped off the kitchen counter and checked his watch for about the hundredth time. What if Kim changed her mind about coming back? He supposed he could eat the entire blueberry pie, to give him an excuse to return his mother's pan. And beg an antacid for his stomach!

He was eyeing the golden crust when he heard

Lulu bark. A car pulled up outside, so he peeked cautiously through the front window.

Kim was sitting behind the wheel of her sassy red coupe with her head bowed. Was she feeling poorly or working up her nerve? Depending on what she said, the next half hour might very well change both their lives.

Swallowing hard, David went outside. "Seat belt stuck?" He was gripping the railing so tightly that his fingers had probably left marks in the wood.

If Kim's heart were to beat any faster, she'd probably break some kind of record. Hearing a familiar voice, she looked up to see the father of her child standing on the porch.

Let me find the right words, she prayed silently as she got out of the car. Her knees trembled when she walked up the steps. On the way over, she had tried to figure out what his reaction would be—anger, disappointment, blame? Guilt?

At least she knew that he liked kids. He would be a good father.

"I made coffee." He flashed a quick grin. "And I just happen to have some fresh blueberry pie baked by a queen and delivered by an angel. How about it?"

If Kim tried to eat, she would gag for sure. "Pie sounds good," she heard herself say as she followed him inside.

"Have a seat while I dish it up." He motioned toward the dining room table. "Still take your coffee black?"

Legs weak, she sank onto the chair. "Uh, no. With milk if you have it." Black coffee made her queasy these days.

She watched him silently as he brought out forks, spoons and a little cream pitcher that matched the fat blue sugar bowl sitting in the middle of the table. As her nervousness grew, he came back with two steaming mugs of coffee. She reached for the milk, but her hand shook so badly that she had to hide it in her lap.

He returned with two plates of pie and set one in front of her.

"I talked to Zane last night." He sat down and stirred sugar into his coffee. "I called him in Bend. Susan says he seems to be adjusting okay. He misses his mom, of course."

"I'm pregnant," Kim blurted before her head could explode with her secret. "I'm sorry. I didn't mean it to happen."

David's hand stilled. "You're sure?"

She forced herself to meet his gaze, expecting to see his face frozen with shock. Sure, it took two, but she was the one who had insisted it would be okay to take a chance.

"Are you feeling all right?" he asked calmly. They might as well be discussing the weather. "No problems so far, not like last time?"

"It hasn't been that long," she reminded him with a stir of resentment. Didn't he even care that they'd made a child together? Her hand pressed against her stomach protectively.

He pushed his pie aside and planted his elbows on the table. "Why are you sorry?"

She gaped at him. "Aren't you? You don't even seem surprised."

"We didn't use protection, so I guess on some

level I knew it was possible. And I've always wanted children of my own.''

''Well, sure,'' she sputtered without thinking, ''but didn't you plan on being married to their mother?''

''You and I could get married.''

Kim couldn't have been more stunned if he had suggested they run away and join a circus as a two-headed clown, but then she realized she should have been prepared for this.

David was an honorable man. No matter how he really felt inside, he would fulfill what he saw as his obligation to her.

''We have other options,'' she argued. ''You don't have to make an honest woman of me.''

He was already shaking his head. ''I know that, but I want our child to have my name.''

''I could lose this baby,'' she reminded him.

Frowning, he lifted his fork and poked at his pie absently. ''Is another miscarriage likely?'' he asked. ''I mean, is there a bigger chance that might happen because of last time?''

She had to be honest. ''Not according to the doctor I saw then. She said if I managed to get pregnant at all, I'd have as good a chance as anyone of carrying it to term.''

''I'm glad.'' He looked utterly sincere.

''Between that and my cycle, I thought it was a safe time,'' she continued apologetically.

''I understand. Now think for a minute, okay? There are a lot of reasons why getting married is a good idea.''

She stuck out her chin. ''Like what? That I'm pregnant?''

''Well, our families, for one.'' He started ticking

the points off his fingers. "We share the ranch. We go to the same church and our backgrounds are similar."

"Of course," she said. "We're both children of divorce."

He frowned at her interruption, but she kept on. "It's more important to me that our baby be surrounded by love than for its parents to be legal. We can raise it without some legal piece of paper binding us together."

"Of course we'll love our baby." He looked appalled. "There's no question of that."

"That's not what I meant." She stared down at her coffee. "I won't raise my child in a marriage where the parents don't love each other. We can work out a fair custody agreement, but that will have to be enough. It's as far as I'm willing to go."

When she lifted her head to see his reaction, she could have sworn that he had gone pale. It must be the overhead light.

Part of her hoped desperately that he would contradict her, that he would drop to one knee and swear that he did love her. Always had, always would.

"Sometimes love grows after a couple gets married," he insisted, looking mulish.

Kim bit the inside of her cheek to keep from sobbing. "If you and I were meant to fall in love, it would have happened by now."

"Sometimes things aren't exactly the ideal way we want them," David retorted, voice rising. "That doesn't mean that we can't make it work."

Kim shook her head, her heart aching with regret. She had handled this badly from the start, but now she had run out of options. "I got married the first time for all the wrong reasons.'' Her voice was husky as she swallowed her tears. ''I promised myself that the next time I won't settle for less than the only *right* reason, and that's love.''

''You're being selfish,'' David said flatly.

Kim took a deep breath. He had a stake in this, too. ''I appreciate your offer.''

''Will you at least think about it a little longer?'' he pleaded, hands fisted on the table. ''This is too important for you to decide the future in five minutes flat. Three lives are at stake.''

She wanted to point out that he had decided to propose in about thirty seconds, right after she'd broken the news, but she didn't bother. ''That's a little dramatic, don't you think?''

''Not at all. Maybe I should have said, for our baby's sake.''

She started to speak, but he raised a hand to deter her. ''No, please don't answer me now. Give it a few days. If you think it would help, we can talk to Mom and Adam. I'll come over and we'll do it together.''

Kim shook her head adamantly. ''No. If we tell them, they'll all gang up on us.''

His face was innocent. ''Why would they, unless they agree that getting married would be the right choice for us?''

''So you think we should just take a vote?'' she asked sarcastically. She was still stung by the practicality of his proposal. ''Simple majority wins? Why stop with the Winchesters? Why not ask the Carltons down the road, or old Mrs. Grubb? How about the Vandermeers at church? Their brood is pretty big.'' She snapped her fingers. ''I know, we could have

Joe Willy poll his customers down at the Longhorn and see what they think.''

''Yeah, yeah, I get the picture. Have you told anyone else besides me?'' David asked, cheeks flushing.

Kim was instantly contrite. It wasn't his fault that he couldn't return her feelings.

''Aunt Robin found out, but that was an accident,'' she admitted. ''She promised not to tell anyone until I'm ready.''

''I?'' he repeated. ''Does she think you were artificially inseminated?''

It was Kim's turn to blush. ''She doesn't know you're the father.''

For a moment he looked angry, but he didn't ask how Robin had found out. Instead he slid back his chair and got to his feet.

''Promise me that you'll really consider getting married, okay?''

She stood up to face him. Not in a million years, she thought. Running into him in the future was going to be difficult enough. Being his wife, knowing he didn't return her feelings, would be a hell she couldn't possibly endure.

''Whatever you say.'' She would have agreed to almost anything, except marriage of course, just to stop him from pressuring her further. ''Thanks for dessert, but I'm not hungry after all.''

''I handled it all wrong.'' David paced the floor of his mother's studio the next morning.

Kim might have refused his suggestion that the two of them ask their parents for advice, but he hadn't promised her that he wouldn't tell anyone the news.

"Would you talk some sense into her?" he pleaded now.

Of course he would never expect his mother to keep a secret this big from her husband. In fact, on the few occasions David could remember seeing Adam lose his temper, she had probably been the only person whose opinion he respected. If *she* leaked the news to him about his daughter's pregnancy, perhaps she would be able to stop him from hunting David down and turning him into a steer with a dull knife.

"Oh, honey," she told David now, "I can't interfere. It's only been since Kim's come back this last time that I've made any progress getting closer. Can you imagine how she'd feel if I got into the middle of this and started offering her unsolicited advice?"

"Who else is there to give her advice, unasked for or not?" David demanded. "Adam?"

His mother's expression was answer enough.

"How about Christie?" he continued ruthlessly. "Maybe Kim could fly over to Italy and ask for her sensible opinion."

"That's not fair!" his mother protested.

"Unless there are some caffeine-swilling, tree-hugging, software-programming girlfriends back in Seattle that she's neglected to mention, she doesn't have anyone else to ask," he replied. "Oh, wait. Maybe Robin will take her over to the women's clinic in Elizabeth. Is that what you want for your grandchild? For its fate to be decided by strangers?"

"Okay, just answer me one thing," his mother said, using the tone she reserved for times she expected compliance. "Do you love her? Not like a sister, not like an old friend, but like she's the only woman in the world you can imagine marrying?''

David stopped his pacing. ''Oh, yeah.'' His voice was hoarse. ''Since I was sixteen.''

''I see.'' His mother reached up to brush aside the hair that had fallen onto his forehead. ''Is that what you want me to tell her?''

He reared back in shock. ''Hell, no! My only shot at success is to get that ring on her finger before she has any idea that I'm crazy about her.''

To his utter stupefaction, his mother tipped back her head and started to laugh.

David folded his arms across his chest and tapped his foot, glaring.

Finally she got control of her hilarity, wiped the tears of mirth from her eyes and reached up to give him a hug. For a moment he remained rigid, offended by her attitude, but then he begrudgingly accepted her embrace.

''What's so funny?'' he demanded after she had let him go. ''Do you find this situation humorous?''

''Of course not,'' she replied. ''I'm just so amazed that you men *ever* succeed in the romance department, given your convoluted thinking when it comes to us poor simple women.''

''Now I really am offended,'' he growled. ''What's wrong with my thinking?''

''Did you listen to yourself?'' she demanded, flinging out her hand. ''If you want her to marry you, what's wrong with telling her how you feel? It seems to me it's the best argument you've got.''

''Not if she doesn't want to hear it!'' When he realized what he'd let slip, his face got hot.

''How do you know that for sure?'' his mother

probed. "Have you told her? No, that would be much too direct."

David remembered the way Kim had acted that wonderful, terrible morning-after, back in the hotel room in L.A. "Trust me, there's no point."

His mother sighed. "Okay, sweetie. I can't promise anything, but I'll do what I can."

When Kim got back from an unusually busy day at the clinic that included a computer crash, several emergencies, a phone that wouldn't stop ringing and one vet being out sick, she sneaked into the house totally wrung out. To her relief the kitchen was empty, so she hurried upstairs to her room for a much-needed nap before dinner.

When she got there, she closed the door and flopped onto her bed. All she had been able to think about, between phone calls, appointments and minor crises, was David's proposal last night. It was a miracle that she'd been able to get any work done. No one had complained, at least not to her, so she must have managed to fake some level of competence.

Stacking her hands under her chin, she weighed all the points for accepting his proposal against the single towering reason she couldn't.

He didn't love her. If he had, surely he might have thought to mention it somewhere in his list of reasons. Even though she wouldn't have believed him, it would have been sweet of him to pretend.

She was about to turn onto her back when there was a soft knock at the door. It was probably Cheyenne, who enjoyed telling Kim about her day.

"I'm resting, sweetie. Can our visit wait until a little later?" she called out.

"Kim? Could I talk to you for a minute?" It was Emily's voice on the other side of the door, not Cheyenne's.

Kim sat up and glanced at the clock. It had become her habit to help her stepmother with dinner while they visited. The more they talked, the more comfortable Kim had become with Emily.

"Be right out. I didn't realize it was so late," Kim said.

She fluffed her hair with her hand and opened the door. "Need some help in the kitchen?"

Emily glanced down the hall. "Actually I was hoping to talk to you privately."

Kim looked at her, cheeks going hot. Emily knew, she realized.

For a moment Kim felt as though her forehead had been branded with a big red *A*.

"Come on in." She opened the door wider and went back over to perch on the edge of the bed so that Emily could take the chair by her desk.

"Have a seat." Damn David for his big mouth.

Emily's brown eyes, so similar to those of her son, were brimming with concern. "How are you feeling?"

No point in beating around the bush, even though Kim felt like squirming. "Fine, considering." She hunched her shoulders and stuck her hands between her knees. "Have you told my father yet?"

Emily shook her head. "I'm hoping you and my son would do that soon."

"So David burned rubber all the way over here this morning to tell you?" Kim demanded, taking the offensive. "He didn't waste much time."

"He asked me to talk to you," Emily admitted.

"I thought you might like to have a woman's perspective, since your mother is in Europe." She started to get up. "If I'm intruding, I'll just go."

"I'm sorry. You're right." Kim motioned for her to stay and then she took a moment to get her emotions under control. "The whole thing is just…"

"Overwhelming?" Emily guessed.

Kim sighed. "Yeah, totally. David wants to get married, but I think it would be one more big mistake."

"It probably would be if you don't love him," Emily agreed.

The unasked question hung in the air between them like a tiny weather balloon.

"I've never told anyone," Kim replied softly. "I've never even said it out loud before."

Emily waited silently, a look of understanding on her delicate face.

"Okay," Kim grumbled. "I love David, but I'm still not going to marry him."

"Mind if I ask why not?"

"It's just not enough." Kim dabbed at her eyes, embarrassed for losing control in front of the woman she used to resent. "Even the baby isn't enough, not unless David loved me, too."

She looked up at the ceiling. "Oh, he'd marry me out of obligation and responsibility, because he's a good guy and he's convinced it's the right thing to do." She swallowed hard and her gaze met Emily's. "Don't you see? It wouldn't be fair, not to him or to me or to…" She pressed her hand to her stomach. "Or to junior."

Emily seemed to be debating. "Can I tell you a little story?"

Kim took a deep, steadying breath. "Sure." She felt foolish for acting like a baby herself.

"You may remember that I first met your father when he came by my house to buy my paltry twenty acres. I thought he'd seen me in town and was hitting on me, but that's another story." She smiled with obvious fondness for the memory. "Anyway, I told him I had no intention of selling, especially not to him, but he wouldn't give up. He needed my water, as well as my land, so he wouldn't give up."

Kim listened, fascinated. When her father and Emily started seeing each other, her own feelings had been too bitter for her to pay attention to what was going on around her.

"Well, the next thing I knew, he claimed to be interested in me." Emily glanced down at her hands. "Of course, there were complications."

"David and me," Kim supplied.

"Well, yes." Emily dismissed the two of them with a flap of her hand. "But more than that was the fact that I found myself falling hard for someone whose motives I didn't completely trust. Was he being honest about his attraction to me, or was this just a new scheme to get what he really wanted?"

"How did you know what to do?" Kim asked, genuinely curious.

"I had no idea. When I agreed to marry your father, it was because of my own feelings, not his."

Kim was surprised by her candid answer. "Are you saying it can work out with love only on one side?" she asked. "Because I know Daddy did love you, almost from the start."

Emily blushed. "Well, thank you, honey. I can't give you all the answers," she admitted. "What I know is that I nearly lost out on the happiest years of my life, just because I was scared to take another chance. I guess what I'm telling you is to trust your instincts and to have faith in your own ability to handle whatever happens. You're stronger than you know.'' She spread her hands in a helpless gesture. ''My other suggestion is for you to ask my son how he feels, and then don't be afraid to accept what he tells you.''

Kim rubbed her forehead with her fingertips. ''You've given me a lot to think about.''

Emily got to her feet. ''Just because David is my son doesn't mean that I'm not on your side, too.''

''Just talking to you has helped a lot, but what about Daddy?'' Kim asked. ''I don't want to be the cause of any problems between you two, so I wouldn't ask you not to tell him.''

Emily took a deep breath. ''I won't say anything to your father without talking to you first, okay?''

Kim smiled. ''Fair enough.''

When David got back from the building supply store on Saturday, there was a note taped to his front door.

''I'd like to talk,'' it said in Kim's loopy handwriting. ''I'll be at the big rock at two.''

David stared at the note. The rock she had mentioned was a boulder in the northeast section, where he and Kim used to meet when they were teenagers.

His heart began to thud. Why had she chosen that particular location? Because it was private and easy to find, or was it some kind of sign?

He glanced at his watch, knowing that each minute until two was going to seem like an hour.

When the time finally crawled closer, he walked out to the rock with Lulu at his side. Even though they got there a little early, Kim's car was already parked at the end of the dirt track.

Lulu ran on ahead, but David followed her almost reluctantly, circling the boulder to the other side where Kim was sitting in the shade. Her appearance never failed to halt his breath. Had he ever told her how beautiful she was?

"I got your note," he said, immediately realizing how inane the remark must sound. Of course he had, or he wouldn't be here, would he?

"I'm glad." With a faint smile, she patted the ground beside her. Lulu had already flopped down in the grass a few feet away. "Have a seat."

He remained standing, braced to debate her, if necessary. "What have you decided?"

"Could we talk for a little while?" she asked. "I'll get a stiff neck if I have to look up at you much longer."

Immediately contrite, he sank down beside her. The idea of kissing her crossed his mind, but he had already realized leaving emotion out of the situation was the wisest way to handle it. Besides, if she thought agreeing to marry him would mean that he expected to paw her whenever he wanted, she might refuse.

"Still feeling okay?" he asked.

She nodded. "Nothing's changed."

Her comment hurt him. Did she think he was hoping she would lose the baby? "You know that's not what I meant."

"I'm sorry." She looked contrite, and he debated offering to pay for her to see a doctor.

If he did, would she view his suggestion as a sign that he cared about her health, or heavy-handed meddling that would only get worse if she said yes? Afraid to make a misstep, he remained silent.

Kim broke off a long blade of grass and fiddled with it for a moment. "I've decided to accept your proposal," she announced without warning.

The suddenness of her statement caught David totally off guard, leaving him speechless with relief. His only regret was that she wasn't accepting for the same reason he had for asking.

He wished he could tell her how much he loved her.

"You won't be sorry," he choked instead. Keeping his feelings hidden until after they tied the knot so she wouldn't bolt was going to be damned difficult, especially around their family. The women, especially, were too damned perceptive to be fooled for long.

"I'll take good care of you and our baby," he vowed. "You won't be sorry."

"I know you will." She studied his face intently, making him wonder just what she saw when she looked at him. "Do you remember when I left to live with my mother in Denver?"

"Of course I do. Your decision took me by surprise." He almost added that she had broken his heart, but he stopped just in time.

"I was hoping you might call or write to me," she admitted, breaking off another blade of grass. A tiny frown pleated the skin between her feathery brows, and her lashes veiled her eyes.

"I did write!" he exclaimed, instantly indignant. "I sent you two letters. When you didn't reply, I called and left a message with your mother. She promised to tell you. When I didn't hear anything back, I didn't know what else to do."

Kim's gaze met his. "I never got your letters, and she didn't tell me you'd called." She bit her lip. "Perhaps she forgot."

"Maybe you're the one who forgot," he argued, losing track of how much was at stake. "I sweated bullets writing those letters."

Kim scooted away from him. "You're wrong," she said flatly. "I know leaving without saying good-bye was thoughtless, but at the time I felt like my father had let me down horribly. Maybe I was testing you, but I always thought you had let me go without a word. That was the real reason I didn't come back when she lost her job at the gallery, the reason I went with her to Seattle instead."

"I loved you!" he cried. "You broke my heart when you left!"

"You never told me," she exclaimed.

"We were young. You seemed so mixed up, and so unhappy about our folks seeing each other." The pain now was much more intense than his disappointment had been then. He knew now just how much he stood to lose.

"Yes, your father probably was too strict and too protective, but I wasn't sure which was more important to you at the time, me or getting back at him. I don't think you knew at the time, either."

She bit her lip. "Maybe you're right, but you have to believe me when I say that I never had any idea that you tried to contact me, I swear."

"Why would your mother do something like that?" he asked.

Kim shrugged. "To keep me from coming home, I suppose. Who knows?" She arranged some pebbles into a circle in the dirt. "It's nice to know that you tried."

"Why did you get married?" It was something David had pondered a hundred times. "Did you love him?"

Her smile was sad. "I thought I did. I guess I was trying to get away from my mother. If I had come back to Colorado, she would have taken it as a personal rejection, but getting married, especially to such a great catch—" her tone was heavily sarcastic "—was an acceptable reason to her."

David wasn't sure he understood, but he knew how frustrated Kim had been by Adam's strict parenting. He hadn't trusted his daughter to make any decisions for herself. Now David could see that Adam's attempt to keep Kim from leaving him, the same way her mother and grandmother had, only brought about the very thing he had tried to avoid. Adam had driven her away.

"Why did you agree to marry me?" David asked. "You're strong enough and smart enough to have this baby by yourself, if that's what you want to do."

She smiled, obviously pleased by the comment.

"You know our parents would help, and so would I," he continued. "I'll still be there for you, even if you truly don't want to marry me."

What the hell was he doing, trying to talk her out of it after she had already agreed? Was he insane?

"Please, wait. I don't, I'm not, I mean—" he stuttered, trying desperately to backtrack.

"It's okay," she interrupted. "To quote a very

wise lady, I'm marrying you because of *my* feelings, not yours.''

His confusion must have shown on his face. ''What wise woman?'' he demanded. ''What are you talking about?''

''If I answer your questions, will you promise to answer one for me?'' she asked.

He bobbed his head, ready to agree to anything. ''Sure.''

Kim took a deep breath. Briefly she squeezed her eyes shut, and when she opened them again, they glistened like diamonds.

David's heart climbed right into his throat. Damn it, all his double talk had changed her mind. If he'd succeeded in losing her again, he was going home to cut out his tongue!

''The wise woman who said that is your mother,'' she continued.

He tried to look innocent. ''When did you talk to her?''

''It doesn't matter.'' She moved another pebble, and then she lifted her head. ''I'm marrying you because I love you.''

All he could do was stare, afraid to move. Afraid to breathe, for fear of waking up from this lovely, lovely dream.

''Not quite the response I was hoping for,'' she said lightly, but her smile wobbled and her cheeks had flushed bright pink.

It was true. He could see it in her eyes. She loved him, truly loved him.

He had just been handed a gift he'd never thought he would receive.

Hand trembling, he cupped her cheek.

"You promised to answer one question for me," she whispered.

"What is it?" He could hardly concentrate, too intent on absorbing what she had just told him. He felt as though he might just fly apart.

"You already know." One lone tear spilled onto his finger.

Suddenly he realized exactly what she was asking.

"Here's my answer." Slowly he leaned down until his mouth was nearly touching hers. "I'm marrying you because you've been the keeper of my heart since high school," he said softly. "You dented it, you broke it. Hell, you rode right over it, but now you've made it whole again."

Kim's arms came up around his neck and he lowered his head until their lips met and clung. He didn't know if it was her heartbeat he felt or his own.

"I've never been so happy," she said when he finally, reluctantly peeled his mouth off hers and let her go. "You have no idea how much you mean to me."

"I'll give you a lifetime to show me," he replied. "Just as I intend to show you, every day for the rest of our lives."

He wanted to kiss her again, but he knew if he did he was in danger of losing control. The pasture wasn't quite private enough for that.

He got to his feet and held out his hands to his future bride.

"Do you think your father will come after me with a shotgun?" he asked, only half kidding.

Flashing him a grin that went straight to his heart, Kim took his hand. "Let's go tell him and find out."

* * * * *

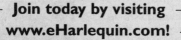

Your opinion is important to us! Please take a few moments to share your thoughts with us about your experiences with Harlequin and Silhouette books. Your comments will be very useful in ensuring that we deliver books you love to read. *Please take a few minutes to complete the questionnaire, then send it to us at the address below.*

Send your completed questionnaires to:
Harlequin/Silhouette Reader Survey, P.O. Box 9046, Buffalo, NY 14269-9046

1. As you may know, there are many different lines under the Harlequin and Silhouette brands. Each of the lines is listed below. Please check the box that most represents your reading habit for each line.

Line	Currently read this line	Do not read this line	Not sure if I read this line
Harlequin American Romance	❑	❑	❑
Harlequin Duets	❑	❑	❑
Harlequin Romance	❑	❑	❑
Harlequin Historicals	❑	❑	❑
Harlequin Superromance	❑	❑	❑
Harlequin Intrigue	❑	❑	❑
Harlequin Presents	❑	❑	❑
Harlequin Temptation	❑	❑	❑
Harlequin Blaze	❑	❑	❑
Silhouette Special Edition	❑	❑	❑
Silhouette Romance	❑	❑	❑
Silhouette Intimate Moments	❑	❑	❑
Silhouette Desire	❑	❑	❑

2. Which of the following best describes why you bought *this book?* One answer only, please.

the picture on the cover	❑	the title	❑
the author	❑	the line is one I read often	❑
part of a miniseries	❑	saw an ad in another book	❑
saw an ad in a magazine/newsletter	❑	a friend told me about it	❑
I borrowed/was given this book	❑	other: _____	❑

3. Where did you buy *this book?* One answer only, please.

at Barnes & Noble	❑	at a grocery store	❑
at Waldenbooks	❑	at a drugstore	❑
at Borders	❑	on eHarlequin.com Web site	❑
at another bookstore	❑	from another Web site	❑
at Wal-Mart	❑	Harlequin/Silhouette Reader	
at Target	❑	Service/through the mail	❑
at Kmart	❑	used books from anywhere	❑
at another department store or mass merchandiser	❑	I borrowed/was given this book	❑

4. On average, how many Harlequin and Silhouette books do you buy at one time?

I buy _____ books at one time	❑
I rarely buy a book	❑

MRQ403SSE-1A

5. How many times per month do you shop for any *Harlequin and/or Silhouette* books?
One answer only, please.

1 or more times a week	❑	a few times per year	❑
1 to 3 times per month	❑	less often than once a year	❑
1 to 2 times every 3 months	❑	never	❑

6. When you think of your ideal heroine, which *one* statement describes her the best?
One answer only, please.

She's a woman who is strong-willed	❑	She's a desirable woman	❑
She's a woman who is needed by others	❑	She's a powerful woman	❑
She's a woman who is taken care of	❑	She's a passionate woman	❑
She's an adventurous woman	❑	She's a sensitive woman	❑

7. The following statements describe types or genres of books that you may be
interested in reading. Pick *up to 2 types* of books that you are most interested in.

I like to read about truly romantic relationships	❑
I like to read stories that are sexy romances	❑
I like to read romantic comedies	❑
I like to read a romantic mystery/suspense	❑
I like to read about romantic adventures	❑
I like to read romance stories that involve family	❑
I like to read about a romance in times or places that I have never seen	❑
Other: _____	❑

*The following questions help us to group your answers with those readers who are
similar to you. Your answers will remain confidential.*

8. Please record your year of birth below.
19 _____

9. What is your marital status?

single ❑   married ❑   common-law ❑   widowed ❑
divorced/separated ❑

10. Do you have children 18 years of age or younger currently living at home?
yes ❑   no ❑

11. Which of the following best describes your employment status?

employed full-time or part-time ❑   homemaker ❑   student ❑
retired ❑   unemployed ❑

12. Do you have access to the Internet from either home or work?
yes ❑   no ❑

13. Have you ever visited eHarlequin.com?
yes ❑   no ❑

14. What state do you live in?
_____

15. Are you a member of Harlequin/Silhouette Reader Service?
yes ❑   Account # _____   no ❑   MRQ403SSE-1B

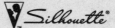

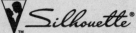

COMING NEXT MONTH

#1567 THE MARRIAGE MEDALLION—Christine Rimmer
Viking Brides
Spirited princess Brit Thorsen traveled far to confront Prince
Eric Greyfell, the one man who may have known her brother's
whereabouts. But Eric recognized the *real* reason fate had sent
Brit to him. She wore the Greyfell marriage medallion plainly
around her neck—marking her as his bride....

#1568 THE RANCHER'S DAUGHTER—Jodi O'Donnell
Montana Mavericks: The Kingsleys
Softhearted Maura Kingsley had a penchant for fix-up projects—
especially when the projects were people! Her latest assignment?
Ash McDonough, the "bad seed" of Rumor, Montana. Ash was
darkly tormented—and incredibly sexy. But good girl Maura wasn't
interested in him. Was she?

#1569 PRACTICE MAKES PREGNANT—Lois Faye Dyer
Manhattan Multiples
Shy, sweet Allison Baker had had one night of impulsive unbridled
passion with attorney Jorge Perez—and she'd ended up pregnant!
Jorge insisted they marry. But theirs would be a marriage of
convenience, not love, despite what Allison's heart wanted to believe!

#1570 SHOULD HAVE BEEN HER CHILD—Stella Bagwell
Men of the West
He hadn't loved her enough to stay. That's what Dr. Victoria Ketchum
believed of her former love Jess Hastings. But Jess was back in
town—with his baby daughter. Could Victoria resist the yearning in
her heart or would temptation lead to a second chance for the reunited
couple?

#1571 SECRETS OF A SMALL TOWN—Patricia Kay
Sabrina March's father's secret had brought her to warm and fun-
loving restaurant owner Gregg Antonelli. But the sins of her parents
kept her from pursuing the heady feelings being with Gregg evoked.
Sabrina's father's legacy of deceit threatened to taint the one love she
had ever known....

#1572 COUNTING ON A COWBOY—Karen Sandler
Single dad Tom Jarret had a problem—his recently suspended nine-
year-old spitfire of a daughter, to be exact. Tom hired stunningly
beautiful teacher Andrea Larson to homeschool his daughter...but
could Andrea's exquisite tenderness teach the jaded rancher how to
love again?

SSECNM0903